Chloë Rayban

Brought up in two lands and two cultures herself, Chloë Rayban has used this experience to draw out the contrasting and universal elements of young love. She was born in England and educated here until the age of seventeen, when her family decided to spend a year in Australia. After attending university in Perth, she returned to take a degree in Philosophy at Newcastle University before working as an advertising copywriter. Chloë now combined freelance copywriting with bringing up a family and writing children's fiction.

Also in the Contents series

Contents

Under Different Stars
CHLOË RAYBAN

mammoth

First published in Great Britain 1988
by Methuen Children's Books Ltd
as *Under Different Stars* by Carolyn Bear
Published 1990 by Teens Mandarin
Reissued 1998 by Mammoth
an imprint of Reed International Books Limited
Michelin House, 81 Fulham Road, London SW3 6RB

ISBN 0 7497 3333 0

10 9 8 7 6 5 4 3 2 1

A CIP catalogue record for this title
is available from the British Library

Printed in Great Britain
by Cox & Wyman Ltd, Reading, Berkshire

Perth, Western Australia
1961

Chapter One

Julia: It was late afternoon on a May day that signalled by the angle of the reclining sun that this was the tail-end of summer. I had taken to walking over the hump-back, scrub-covered hillock that separated the University from the city. By careful timing I could always catch that precise moment when the low light spilling across the surface of the Swan River turned the water into an opaque sheet of milky pearl. In the distance the city would be smudged into an untidy blue grey line that slowly and imperceptibly merged into the gathering dusk. By the time I descended into the suburbs at the far side of the park, the first string of street lights would be flickering to life along the swinging arc of the slip-road that led up to the Causeway.

This was a route I had been strongly advised not to take. It was hard to tell if this added to or detracted from the enjoyment.

On this particular day I walked more slowly than usual, carrying a heavy bag of books and savouring that time that divided the hours of daytime note-taking from the hours of reluctant, but necessary, study in the evening. On reaching the high-point where the path turned away from the University and skirted the outcrop that looked out over the river, I glanced back automatically and noticed with slight irritation that there was someone else coming up the hillside.

He was tall, and walked with a long loose-limbed stride that meant he would soon catch up with me. I

7

quickened my pace and as I reached the loneliest part of the path, I started to wonder whether I shouldn't have taken my parents' advice after all. I glanced over my shoulder again. He was shabby and the laces of his dirty canvas shoes trailed in the dust. The little hairs on the back of my neck were pricking up with apprehension. I clung on to my bag as tightly as I could. If anything happened I knew it would be totally my own fault.

By the time I rounded the bend where the city came into view, I could hear the soft dust-muffled sound of his footsteps very close behind me. The faster I walked, the faster he followed.

Quite suddenly I felt anger flush through me. Why on earth should I not be free to walk where I liked, when I liked? I swung round.

'You're following me!' I accused him.

'Yes, I am,' he replied. I was relieved to see that he was hardly older than me, nineteen perhaps. His clothes were old and unironed and of that uniform sort of grey-khaki that comes from being washed with everything else too many times. Under his arm he carried a battered file. Scrawled over it I could just make out the word 'Metaphysics'.

'Why are you following me?' I demanded.

'You were in front of me. I was behind you. On a path like this it's virtually inevitable,' he replied.

We walked on uncomfortably, in single file for some moments.

Then we came to the place where the path widened and the city came into view.

'Wouldn't it be better if I walked along with you?' he said. 'After all, we are going the same way.'

'All right,' I replied awkwardly.

'Shall I carry that bag for you?'

I eyed him narrowly. Even the subtlest sort of mugger was unlikely to be carrying a file marked

8

'Metaphysics'. However, it was best to err on the safe side.

'No, thank you, I can manage.'

We walked on in silence for some distance. Then, quite suddenly, the sky and the river put on a real virtuoso performance staining the surface of the water with flamingo colours. And he just stopped right there in the middle of the path and stood staring at it.

Then, equally abruptly, he started walking again with that long loping stride of his and I found I was hurrying to keep up with him.

'S'pose you don't have corny sunsets like that where you come from?' he said.

'How do you know where I come from?'

He didn't answer.

'Where are you going anyway?' I asked.

'Same as you,' he answered.

'Oh, and where's that?'

'No idea. Where are we going?'

'So you *were* following me!'

'That's what I said.'

'Look,' I replied firmly, 'I'm going home. I've got work to do.' I shifted the heavy bag on to the other shoulder.

'I wish you'd let me carry that,' he said. 'It's only a pile of old books, after all.'

'All right, carry it then,' I handed the bag over.

'Do you mean to say you carry this lot home every night?' he asked.

'Not every night,' I answered.

'Oh no, that's right. On Tuesdays you don't come this way, do you?'

'Look. Are you some kind of freak or loony or something? How do you know what I do? I've never seen you before in my life.'

9

We were entering the first row of neat houses or 'homes' as they were called, in the suburb.

A sun-bronzed young housewife was hanging clothes on her circular dryer. She paused and stared at us as she heard my raised voice.

'Do you mind keeping your voice down?' he said. 'This is a nice neighbourhood.'

The prim respectable windows of the street gazed blankly at us.

'Hand me that bag. Now would you please just go away and leave me alone!'

He swung the bag over to me and watched as I took it and began to stride off with as much dignity as I could, despite its weight.

I traced my way through the few side streets that led down to where my bus stopped. I could tell he was still following me, hands in pockets, with that long unhurried stride of his, but I pretended he wasn't there.

By the time I reached the bus stop it was quite dark and I was glad to see that there was already quite a number of people waiting there. I lined up behind them. I could sense that he was standing behind me in the queue.

'Look,' I started in a hoarse whisper. 'Will you please go away?'

A woman of vast proportions in front of me, turned and gave us both a searching look.

'I'm only waiting for my bus,' he replied. 'It's a free country, isn't it?'

Two further members of the queue turned and examined us briefly.

To my relief, my bus hauled into sight at that moment, skittering over the tram lines and sending a shower of sparks from its overhead cable into the darkening sky.

I climbed on board. He followed.

'Oh no, no, you're not coming with me.' I turned as if to stop him.

'Look, for Crissake, this is my bus!' he objected.

I felt chastened. I made my way along the bus under the scrutiny of the other passengers, selecting a seat beside the shelf-bosomed woman who had been in front of me in the queue.

He sat down a couple of rows in front of us. As the bus jerked into motion I took out a book and tried to maintain a dignified air of detachment.

Despite myself, I was curious to see where he would get off, but he seemed to have settled back in his seat as if he were anticipating a longish journey. His hair, as nondescript a mouse colour as his clothes, was cut too short so that his pink-rimmed ears stuck out and at the crown of his head a tuft stood on end giving him an absurdly boyish appearance.

He turned at that moment and caught my eye and despite myself I smiled. He didn't smile back, he just settled himself contentedly deeper into his seat. I frowned and concentrated on my book.

The ticket collector was working his way down the bus. He reached my 'companion', who turned and pointed me out.

I felt a little flattered, although I knew I shouldn't allow him to pay for my ticket. He looked hard up and besides, I reminded myself, I didn't even know him.

But after a minute or so I looked up to find the ticket collector leaning over me.

'Fares, please,' he demanded.

I raked in my bag and asked for a ticket to Floreat Park.

'What about him?' asked the collector, jerking his head in 'his' direction.

'What about him?' I asked.

11

'He says he's with you.' The ticket collector was a large man. The collar of his regulation shirt was too tight. Where it rubbed he had a red mark on his neck and as he became agitated this part flushed redder.

'He most certainly isn't with me,' I objected.

The collector turned back to 'him': 'Look, mate. The lady says you're not with her. Come on, give us your fare or you'd better get out and walk.'

'I haven't any money,' he replied with total unconcern.

The conductor moved heavily down to the front of the bus and had a word with the driver. The bus drew into the kerb and lurched to a halt.

'Don't you try and be funny with me. This is where you get off. Either pay up or get off, there's blokes on this bus that want to get home.'

'You can't make me get out,' he said firmly and he hunched himself down in his seat to demonstrate that he meant to stay put.

'I'll have to take your name and address then,' said the conductor, taking out his pad and licking his pencil in a resigned manner.

'What if I refuse to give it to you?' he replied.

A woman two rows down, turned and looked at me accusingly:

'He was with her. I saw them get on together.'

A small tired-looking man, his face ingrained with workday grease, added: 'Come on, pay up for him, love. Even if you've had a tiff it'll all blow over. Then we can all get home.'

'Don't you pay for him,' said the fat woman beside me. 'He was bothering her, I saw. Don't you pay out a penny for the bastards, they'll all take what they can get. Go on, throw him off the bus.'

This seemed to give the general signal for everyone to come out with an opinion for or against me paying up.

I could feel myself blushing from all the attention focused on us.

'Oh look, how much is your beastly fare?' I asked him. It was hardly worth keeping a whole busload of people stranded for the sake of a few pence.

'I'm going to the same place she's going,' he told the conductor.

The fat woman decided that she'd had enough; She rocked to her feet and gathered her bags muttering in protest, then lurched down the aisle complaining loudly about louts and the lack of law and order.

He was standing over me.

'Move up then.' He sank into the seat beside me.

'Haven't you really got any money?' I asked.

He felt deep into his pockets and brought out a couple of pence. 'Want it?' he asked.

'How were you going to get home then?'

'Guess I would have walked.'

'What, all the way to Floreat Park?'

'No, I live in Sinclair Street.'

'Where's that?'

"Bout two stops back.'

'Why the hell didn't you get out?'

'I said I was taking you home.'

'Taking me home!' I like that! It was me who paid your fare.'

'It was I.'

'All right, it was I. I was the one who paid.'

'Look, you're not going to get mean about a few lousy pence. OK, I'll pay you back.'

'It's not the money, you idiot. You're not coming with me.'

'Looks like I am, to me.'

'You're impossible. You really are impossible.' I opened my book and decided to ignore him.

'You've read that sentence three times.'

'So what?'

13

'Do you find my presence disturbs you?'

'No, yes . . . Yes it does, as a matter of fact.'

'That's because you lack self-confidence.'

'Well, that's certainly nothing anyone can accuse you of.'

'It's not a matter of confidence. I've just stopped caring what anyone thinks, that's all. You see I'm a solipsist.'

'A what?'

'A solipsist. A solipsist is a person who doesn't believe in the independent existence of the outside world, other people, that sort of thing.'

'In that case, since I don't exist, you might as well get off this bus and stop pestering me.'

'Yes, but it doesn't work like that. You may well be just an illusion, but then so is everything else, so in the long run it doesn't make any difference. In which case I might as well just go along with you as do anything else.'

'You're mad. You are absolutely mad.'

'If you don't mind me saying so, that's a very clichéd response.'

I stared out of the window. The bus route passed predictable block after block of suburban streets neatly laid out grid-fashion, their front yards identically planted with elephant grass and broad flat-leaved succulents. He was undoubtedly the most unexpected person I had met in the whole of this oddly-familiar foreign country.

'What's your name?' I asked. 'If it's not too clichéd to asked.'

'It's Zig,' he said. And he held out a brown hand and shook mine in a formal continental manner.

'No one's called Zig.'

'I am.'

'Mine's Julia.'

'I know.'

14

'How do you know?'

'I asked people.'

'What people?'

'Just people.'

'You can't really be called Zig.'

'Yes, I am. Lots of people are called Zig where I come from.'

'Where's that?'

'Poland.'

'I didn't think you were Australian.'

The bus had begun its ascent into the neater, more affluent outer suburbs. I gazed out of the window, lost for anything further to say, wondering what on earth was going to happen when we arrived at my stop.

We reached the turnabout at the top of Floreat Park. It was the end of the bus route where the bus swung round and headed back into town, a dusty barren place where the telegraph poles stood at odd angles like the remnants of some drunken forest.

'This is where I get out.'

He followed me down the steps of the bus and I didn't object. We watched it lurch off, casting light from its windows across the neat row of lawns.

I hoisted my bag on to my shoulder and set off down the street. And he came too, kicking a pebble, down to the house my parents had rented.

It was a modern, low-built building of white-washed brick. Outside, it had a single row of plantains which swished uneasily in the sea-breeze that came up at night and gave the house a tropical quality. All through the hot summer nights I had listened to the sound of these plantains and fantasised that beyond the mosquito-wired windows, instead of the neat respectability of Floreat Park, I would find myself on the wilder shores of some hurricane-tossed island.

These day-dreams, night-dreams, waking-dreams,

would include the occasional hero. Sun-bronzed, and mature, he would throw open the door of a gleaming convertible and take me off to some place where we could dance . . .

Zig and I stood outside the house. The plantains rustled. The woman next door threw the slops over her dahlias.

'All right, so you've seen me home. Thank you and goodbye.'

'Aren't you going to ask me in?'

'No, I'm not. Look, I don't even know you.'

'You mean we haven't been officially introduced.' There was an edge of sarcasm in his voice.

'I said I don't know you.'

'So you're expecting me to walk all the way back to Sinclair Street, when I've come all this way just to see you home.'

'OK. Here you are,' I scrabbled for my purse. 'Here's your fare back.'

'This is mighty kind of you, Ma'am. By the way, does it make you feel good, handing out charity?'

I could feel myself flushing with anger. 'You've really got a nerve. Honestly . . .'

A voice came from inside the house. My mother's, questioning: 'Julia, is that you? Have you got some-one with you?'

'Hello, Mummy. Yes, it's me. He's just going, he's got to catch a bus.'

My mother appeared at the door.

'Hello. But, darling, he's just missed the bus. I saw it go down the hill. There won't be another one for at least an hour.'

Zig looked at her, disarmingly embarrassed.

'Well, you'd better come in. You don't want to stand around for an hour at the bus stop.'

'Mummy . . .!'

'What is it, darling?'

'It's just, I've got so much work to do.' She missed my meaningful look. She was too busy ushering Zig in.

'This is very kind of you, Mrs . . .'

'Oh, do call me Daphne and this is Henry.'

My father rose to his feet, welcoming Zig with an outstretched hand.

Zig was greeted like a long-lost friend. The television was turned off, a chair was drawn up. The standard questions were asked: Well, are you at the University? Which year? So what are you studying?

'Philosophy, sir.'

'Sir!', he was really buttering my father up.

'Oh philosophy, eh. How very interesting.'

I couldn't believe it. There he was wiping his filthy sneakers on our doormat. Settling down in the one other armchair. My father was giving him a beer. Soon they were deep in conversation.

I put my books away, combed my hair, washed my face, changed my clothes, and then, since he still hadn't left, sat on a hard dining chair listening to them.

Zig turned to me. 'If you've got tons of study to do, go ahead. I don't want to hold you up or anything.'

'Actually,' I said with dignity. 'I'm going to study later on. When you've gone.' I added meaningfully. In fact, I was ravenous, I couldn't face getting down to studying until I had had my supper.

My mother was trying to attract my attention from the kitchenette. I went out to her. She was holding a saucepan of boiled potatoes.

She mouthed so as not to be heard in the next room: 'Shall I invite him to dinner?'

'NO,' I mouthed emphatically.

Zig's face appeared at the kitchen door. He observed the saucepan. Then, as if the thought had

17

just occurred to him, polite, concerned, he said: 'Look, you folks will want to get on with your meal. Please don't mind me . . .'

'It's only chops,' said my mother. 'But you're more than welcome to join us. You must be hungry . . .'

'Well, if it's really not putting you out. I mean me turning up like this and . . .'

'Nonsense,' said my mother. 'Any friend of Julia's is welcome here.'

I glared at my mother. Zig disappeared to refill his glass from the can my father was holding out.

'But he's not a friend of mine,' I hissed in a stage whisper.

'Then what is he doing here?' whispered my mother.

'He just kind of followed me . . .'

'What do you mean. Followed you? Where?'

There it was. I couldn't explain about walking through the park.

'Oh never mind.'

I found the meal intensely embarrassing. My mother and I had our measly half chop each. Zig had a whole chop, *my* chop, and second and third helpings of vegetables. My mother kept shooting him suspicious glances as if he were a rapist or something. My father kept refilling his glass. They were having an intense conversation about Marxism. I could tell that my father was getting a little out of his depth by the length of the words he was using.

We were just getting on to the pudding when I looked at my watch and realised that Zig had missed the eight-fifteen bus as well.

When I pointed this out, my father said not to worry as he would be quite happy to run Zig back later in the car. My mother and I exchanged despairing glances.

When the meal was finished, Zig started to help

my mother with the washing-up, which let me off, so I went to my room to get on with the vital essay that was due in the next day. I finished at around ten-thirty and I came out to find Zig still deep in conversation.

'But at that time the Church was still arguing about how many angels could dance on the head of a needle . . .'

'That's just what I mean,' said my father. 'The Jesuits who taught me . . .'

I hovered for a moment and then interrupted.

'Don't you think you should be getting back?' I asked Zig. 'Won't someone be wondering where you've got to?'

'Oh no, I very much doubt it,' he answered. 'Has anyone got the time? Oh dear, looks like I've missed the last bus then.'

So my father ran him home. My mother and I were left clearing up the room before bed.

'What a curious young man,' said my mother.

'It's nothing to do with me,' I said defensively. 'You invited him in.'

'Actually I rather liked him,' said my mother. 'He told me all about his childhood. They lived in refugee camps you know. How they must have suffered.'

'Hmmmph,' was my only comment.

'You never did tell me where you met him.'

Chapter Two

Zig: There she was again, walking with that tight-arsed, stuck-up sort of way as if she didn't give a damn about anyone. Which was kind of what intrigued me, because I thought maybe that's something we just might have in common.

Or maybe it wasn't that. Maybe, although I didn't want to admit it at the time, that long heavy dark hair reminded me of Su. And yes, when I come to think of it, there was something slightly Asiatic about her.

And I kept seeing her, and when I did it was like feeling the tug of a wound that had been stitched, reminding me. And I knew that until I had spoken to her, I wasn't going to be able to exorcize the belief that if I got to know her she might be all those things I thought Su-Yen was and I was so wrong about.

Anyway, ever since Su-Yen, I had given up caring. The whole thing had kind of anaesthetized whatever part of my damn mind I was meant to feel with. In a curious sort of way it was a liberating sensation, I could say what I liked to anyone, do what I liked. Whatever happened I didn't damn well feel a thing.

So when I saw that tight-arse of hers making its way up the hill through King's Park, I just followed it. It was on my way home, after all.

When she got to the steep part of the path, she kind of put on steam. In fact, it was quite an effort to keep up. I could feel my shirt getting damp under the arms, which was a drag because I'd been out of deodorant for over a week, and although I didn't give a damn what the creature thought of me, it kind of shakes your confidence to know you're not smelling your best.

By the time we got to the top of the rise that bag of hers was being a bit of a handicap so I caught up pretty quickly.

I was just trying to put together a really cool opening gambit when she turned on me.

'You're following me.'

Close up, she was not as good-looking as I thought. That big-eyed look was mostly make-up, which was smudgy, the way girls get towards the end of the day.

Once we had established prior claim to the path and just who had a right to walk on it – all negotiated in those immaculately snooty English vowels, she grudgingly moved over and I walked beside her for a while.

Then the sun set, spewing out colour all over the sky, which the clouds kind of mopped up turning that corny kind of pink, and the river joined in doubling up the show. And I stood and watched and thought with my usual satisfaction – that's another sodding day nearer the grave.

She looked kind of hunched under that bag of books, so I offered to carry it, and I could see from the way she looked at me that she thought I was going to make off with it or something. A bag of old textbooks!

Then I suddenly realised that she was scared of me. She actually thought I might be going to make a grab for her or something. Women! The arrogance of them!

When we got into the suburbs she relaxed a bit and told me to get lost, which was the kind of reaction I would have expected. But I just followed her all the same because she happened to be going in my direction.

She made her way through the streets walking in the kind of arse-waggling long-legged way girls do when they know you're watching them.

By this time I was really enjoying myself and that was a feeling I hadn't had for weeks. I could tell I was actually getting through to her. It was a good feeling.

As fate had it, she got in the queue at my bus stop. So

the game could continue with no further effort from me all the way home. I felt in my pocket and then I remembered that I'd given my last change away to Bragge for the bet we'd had on the Swedish girl. So what?

Then, the cheek of it, she tried to stop me getting on my bus! She chose a seat purposely beside this great heaving mountain of a woman, who looked like she was pregnant but was past it. So I couldn't sit beside her which was a pity.

When we were a couple of stops down the road I took a look to see if she was still there and she smiled. So I thought, that's OK, she'll probably pay up for me if I sit tight.

It was then the thought occurred to me that this wonderful, heady, world-embracing feeling of simply not giving a damn was just what a solipsist must feel like. And if I just hung on in there, I could confound all those mealy-mouthed old sages who said it was a totally untenable position.

There was a hell of a fuss about the measly nine pence my fare cost. To think that a well-heeled girl like that could be so damn mean! But I just sat and let it all wash over me. It was like getting caught in one of those waves, those big dumpers that come sweeping into the coast and just take you up inside them and swing you over and then throw you up on the beach.

So when she'd paid up, I thought I had better go and give the girl a break and sit beside her and look grateful for her miserly grudging ninepence.

That's when I missed my stop.

'How were you going to get home then?' she asked in a matter-of-fact sort of voice.

'Guess I would have walked.'

'What all the way to Floreat Park?' It killed me the way she said Floreat Park. It sounded like some kind of garden party the way she said it – Flooreat Park.

I started to wonder what sort of home she came from in

22

'Flooreat Park', and come to think of it I didn't have anything better to do that night. In fact I didn't have anything better to do any night. Except my dissertation and this was as good a reason as any to give that a miss, so I said, 'I'm taking you home.'

That flattered her. She suppressed one of those self-satisfied little half-smiles, the way girls do when they think you fancy them.

So I decided to torment her a bit because I liked the way she looked when she was angry.

I told her I was a solipsist as well. That was to test her out in case she was thick. If there's one thing I can't stand it's dim women.

She passed on two counts. First of all she didn't pretend that she knew what a solipsist was. And secondly she made an almost witty comment.

I was really enjoying myself now. I thought with satisfaction how in the morning I would tell Bragge that I'd got all the way home with the ice-maiden.

Then we got to the house. A slight set-back. She lived with her parents. I wasn't prepared for that. Parents had just not entered into the whole scenario.

So I put on my very best being-nice-to-parents manners. I even called the old man 'sir'.

That's the funny thing about it. They were really cool parents. There was none of the typical parental 'What are you doing with my daughter' atmosphere. It was all, 'I'm Daphne and this is Henry'.

Then, before you knew it, there I was with a nice cool beer in the paw, sorting out some of Henry's misconceptions about Marxism. Imagine, an upper-class Englishman with leftist leanings!

She went and washed all that make-up off her face and I couldn't help noticing she didn't look too bad. It made me think of what she would look like when she woke up first thing in the morning, and for a moment that almost put me

23

off my stroke and Henry won a point in the argument totally undeservedly.

It was very peaceful in that little house of theirs. I was nicely settled into an easy chair that rocked slightly if you tipped it up and there were good smells and promising noises coming from the kitchen.

I enjoyed watching the girl too. She had put on something shorter that showed more nicely shaven leg. I wasn't going to get ousted from this very comfortable position. Not if I could avoid it.

So when the kitchen noises got to a really critical-sounding phase I just wandered over to see if I could lend a hand and, surprise, surprise, Daphne invited me to dinner!

I don't think Julia was too happy about that because as soon as she had finished her meal – she didn't eat much but I suppose she was on a diet or something, women generally are – she just pushed off and said she had work to do. Pretty inhospitable if you ask me. But perhaps she felt we'd been leaving her out of the conversation.

Anyway, Daphne came out bearing a tea-towel and handed it to me and told me to dry up for her. In spite of the fact that I was a guest!

'So how did you come to have a name like Zig?' she asked.

I told her I was Polish and she asked some intelligent questions about how we came to be in Australia and what had happened to my parents.

So it all came out, the corny old story of my childhood, I mean. Travelling in that blind drift South from transit camp to transit camp. Mostly just the very old, or the very young, reduced to that fanatical state induced by lack of food, lack of sleep, constant uncertainty – an ever-diminishing band of glazed-eyed drifters, our few belongings in a closely guarded bundle, treasures that were gradually bartered away, so the bundle became lighter and lighter until we arrived on this dry old alien land with nothing left.

'There's no need to feel sorry for me. About my parents, I

24

mean,' I told her, because she was putting on that poor orphan face. 'I never knew them and I've got my grandmother.'

'But she must be a very different generation,' she observed.

'She's not that ancient. But she is very different because she's Polish.'

'So how long have you known Julia?' she asked a propos of nothing. 'Careful of that dish, it looks expensive.'

'Seems like ages,' I replied vaguely. There's something about the shared activity of washing up that makes dangerously for soul-searching. And I had some tricky moments as we skirted around some of the things I should have learned from my *long* friendship with Julia.

After dinner we had ridiculously small cups of black coffee. Julia still seemed busy with her essay, or was she sulking? I hung around for a bit to find out. Which meant I missed the last bus.

So Henry ran me home.

'Tell me, where did you meet Julia?'

'In King's Park. You know the footpath that leads through to the city?'

'Ah huh,' said Henry.

Chapter Three

Julia: I didn't see Zig again for quite some time. I would scan through any crowd I saw at the University, but he never seemed to be there. I never saw him going in or out of the Philosophy Department. In fact, I started to wonder whether perhaps the whole story about him being a student might be some kind of fiction he had made up.

So after a while I started to ask people about him. None of my fellow first-year students had heard of him and I realised I didn't even know his surname. Then one day I came across an American girl I had met at a party. She was in her third year and Philosophy was one of the units she was taking.

'Oh him! He's really weird. How do you know him?' She sucked on the straw of her passion fruit milk shake and eyed me inquisitively.

'We just met, around the campus.'

'He's a real brain-box you know. They reckon he might get a First. And no one but no one gets a First in Philosophy.'

'He didn't seem particularly brilliant to me. Bit of a show-off if you like. Why do you say he's weird?'

'He doesn't go around with the other students. Like he's got no friends. He's never dated any of the girls in our year.'

I thought for a moment: 'Perhaps he hasn't got much money.'

'Perhaps he's, you know . . . prefers guys?'

'No, I don't think so. He doesn't care enough about the way he looks for a start.'

'I should say not. Have you seen the dreadful things he wears and the way he gets his hair cut. Say, you don't have a thing about him or anything, do you?'

'Don't be stupid. You know I'm meant to be Paul's girl, *la grande passion*!' I said lightly.

'Oh sure. You heard from him lately?'

'He writes.' I was evasive. I didn't want to talk about Paul, he was . . . special.

'OK. So if I bump into this freak, you want me to give him a message or anything?'

I hesitated. 'Not really.' Then I added, 'Only he owes me a couple of bus rides. But I don't think he'd be interested anyway.'

I had stopped walking back through the park. The experience of being followed had given me a chastening insight into what might have happened. Besides the weather had become unpredictable, the Australian winter reminding me of the showery weather we had back in England.

But every night on the way home I passed Sinclair Street. I had picked it out on the street map and soon pin-pointed where it was on my route. From the brief glimpse I caught as the bus went by, I could see it was a poor street. Many of the houses still had roofs of painted corrugated iron. The front yards were neglected and children and animals played noisily in the street. It was different from the neat respectability of Floreat Park.

I started to wonder whether, in his mocking way, picking up a well-heeled English girl like me might not have been some kind of introverted practical joke. In time I convinced myself that this seemed the most obvious explanation, so I put the whole thing to the back of my mind and started to concentrate on the study programme I'd have to keep to if I was going to pass my end of year exams.

One afternoon I was alone in the house, struggling to encapsulate the main themes of King Lear into chunks of manageable enough to regurgitate in the English exam. I had been left in charge of my sister's baby, the reason incidentally, for the long trek my parents and I had made to this side of the globe. My mother had insisted on being nearby for the birth of her first grandchild.

The house was still. The plantains swished enticingly outside. The baby, secure in her immaculate English carriage pram, slept in the garden. I had just come to the scene on the moor where the play reaches its climax as Lear and the Fool battle with the elements, when the baby woke up.

I left her for a few minutes making those sort of trial cries that occasionally subside as the child falls back to sleep again. But the storm and the baby appeared to have set in seriously and together were working themselves to a real crescendo.

Then, abruptly, the baby stopped crying. I waited for a moment. Had she gone back to sleep? Then I wondered, what if she had choked? Babies could choke to death. What if I had left her too long?

I hurried guiltily out to the garden.

At the first sight of the pram my blood froze. The covers were thrown back and the baby had gone.

There, standing beside the pram, holding her in his arms, was Zig.

'What are you doing with my sister's baby?' I gasped. 'Give her to me.'

I ran down the steps and grasped the child. Zig handed her over very gently. The baby lay in my arms gurgling at him.

'She's wet. She needs changing, that's the problem,' he observed in a knowledgeable way.

'What do you know about it? You can't just come barging in here picking up people's babies. How did you get in anyhow?' I asked.

'The gate was open,' he said, indicating the tall slatted gate which separated the front garden from the back. My sister must have forgotten to close it when she brought the pram in.

'This baby was in some distress. It's quite wrong to leave babies crying, you know. It can be a very traumatic experience for them.'

'Well, if you know so much about babies, you can help me change her,' I announced.

He stood by like a lamb, handing me safety pins and talcum powder while I inexpertly fumbled with the nappy.

'You're not very good at this, are you?' he said when the baby was back up the right way.

'I thought I did rather well,' I said. The baby, however, had begun to cry again.

'Probably wants a drink,' he said.

I looked at the child doubtfully. My sister had left a bottle of milk which had to be warmed to the right temperature. A tricky business.

I hesitated in the kitchenette, the bottle of cold sterile milk in one hand, the saucepan in the other. Zig watched through the living-room door.

'You're meant to stand the bottle in boiling water.'

'I think I can manage, thank you,' I replied with dignity.

At length, the baby was fed and returned to the pram to sleep. Zig settled himself down on the old cane rocker on the verandah.

'Would you like some tea or something?' I asked.

'Tea? How terribly British of you. No, I don't think so.'

The baby slept. The breeze barely disturbed the long fronds of willow that fell around the pram. The old rocker creaked rhythmically and at the back of my mind the thought nagged away, that I should be working for the English exam.

At length I said: 'I should be working right now.'

'You know something? You're in danger of becoming a really boring swot,' said Zig complacently.

'Look, I didn't ask you to come round here. As a matter of fact I've got a very important English exam on Tuesday. And I really must do some work.'

I stood up to give emphasis to what I said.

'Well, I'm really comfortable here. You go ahead, I won't feel neglected in the least.' Zig leant back and closed his eyes.

'You can't just sit here all day,' I replied crossly. 'Why have you come, anyway?'

'Oh, did I have to have a reason?' Zig felt in his pocket, 'I owe you some money. I came to pay you back.'

'Money? What for?'

'Bus fares.'

'Oh for goodness' sake. Don't be ridiculous.'

'That American friend of yours, the one with the boobs, she said . . .'

'Oh, don't be silly, that was a joke.'

Zig put the coins back in his pocket and continued to rock contentedly.

'But seriously, I think it's about time you left, I really do.'

Zig gazed at me through half-closed eyes. Those slanting slavic eyes of his that gave so little away.

'I bother you, don't I? Me being here bothers you, doesn't it?'

'No it doesn't,' I replied defensively. 'But in general, if people are going to drop in they have the thoughtfulness to call first.'

'How very proper.'

'Look. I'm asking you to leave. Is that clear enough for you?'

Very slowly Zig climbed out of the rocker. He made his way down the veranda steps. At their foot, he turned: 'Do you think you can cope on your own with that baby now?'

'Yes, thank you.'

I followed him across the lawn.

'Goodbye, Zig.'

He went through the tall white slatted gate and I closed it and quietly bolted it behind him.

He stood for a moment the other side. His back to me.

'I wondered if you might like to go and see a film or something.'

'Thank you, but I've got exams. Mocks for those end-of-year things. I'm not going out anywhere until they're finished.' I was glad to have them as an excuse.

'When do they finish?'

'Oh, next Tuesday, I think.'

'OK, so I'll come over Tuesday night and we could maybe go down to a cinema in town.'

'Look, Zig.' It was difficult to say this, but I somehow felt it had to be said right then, I was glad of the gate between us. 'I'm kind of committed to someone. He's not here right now, he's gone to the Eastern States. But I'm going over there in a couple of months and . . .'

'I was only asking you out to a film. I wasn't asking you to sleep with me or anything.' The way he said it was crude.

'I didn't think you were,' I replied coldly.

'Right. So we've got that straight. I'll be over on Tuesday night round seven-ish.'

He strolled away across the front lawn, then, as he reached the roadside he paused and turned back.

'By the way, do you sleep with him?'

'That has absolutely nothing to do with you,' I returned hotly.

'Don't know why you want to get so het up about it,' he went on in a matter-of-fact sort of voice.

'Well, I know why I'm getting het up about it. Because you bloody well get on my nerves. Why don't you just . . . just . . .'

'Go?'

'Exactly. And don't damn well come back, ever!'

'I'm on my way.'

I stormed back into the house, tears of fury rising in my eyes. I was just trying to focus on the fourth act of *King Lear* when the baby started crying again.

The days that followed seemed to merge one into the other as relentless hours of revision were interspersed by the tension of exams. These, in turn, were followed by the restless anxiety of going over in my mind what I had written and what I had left unwritten. It was a bleak time and the greyness of the days was only relieved by two eagerly-opened letters from Paul and one blissful telephone call, the night before the English exam.

I went to bed warm with his reassurance that I was bound to pass. I spent the next morning in the University Library making up for that lost afternoon, when I should have been studying *Lear*, with a final illicit late-late mega-swot. Ignoring dire warnings about the dangers of last minute revision, I took out every single crit-book I could find on *Lear* and systematically worked through the lot.

It was impossible to tell if the exam that afternoon went well or badly. I was so saturated with other people's opinions on the play that as I travelled home that evening, I found it hard to distingush between what I had written and what I had read. I tried to put the whole thing out of my mind and began to look forward to a long bath and a lazy evening in front of the television. I didn't care what trash might be on.

I bathed slowly and luxuriously and then, wrapping my hair in a towel, I rubbed a space clear in the steamed-up bathroom mirror. It seemed like weeks since I had looked at myself properly. The pressure of work had brought on a crop of spots and I dabbed on Clearasil crossly. I looked a wreck. I was glad Paul wasn't around to see me like this.

Bit by bit I felt all the pleasure of having finished the exams ebb away. Suddenly the next two months, the time before I would go East, stretched ahead of me, empty and lonely. And there were more exams ahead, real end-of-year University ones this time.

My thoughts were interrupted by my mother banging on the bathroom door.

'There's someone to see you.'

'Paul,' I immediately thought. Somehow, impossibly, he had managed to get some leave.

'Who?'

'That Polish friend of yours. You know, thingee.'

My mother never could remember names.

'Zig?'

'Well, what shall I do? He seems to think you're going out with him.'

'Tell him to go away.'

'Oh, I can't do that, darling. He's come all the way up here. You'll have to talk to him.'

Wearily I dressed and towel-dried my hair. I dragged a comb through it and thought despondently how dreadful it was going to look if I didn't blow-dry it properly. I smudged on a bit of make-up. I really didn't care how I looked.

Zig was standing in the sitting room gazing out of the window, a can of my father's beer in one hand and a glass in the other.

'Hello,' I said.

He half-turned. The expression on his face was . . . sheepish.

'I thought we had a date,' he said.

At that point my mother bustled into the room.

'Well, you're not taking my daughter out looking like that,' she announced. 'Just look at you. You haven't even shaved.'

It was true; he had about four days' growth of beard and his clothes looked as if he'd slept in them.

'I've been writing my dissertation,' he said by way of explanation.

'Well, that doesn't stop you shaving, does it?' answered my mother. 'Come with me. You can use Henry's razor, I've put a new blade in for you.'

'But Mummy . . .'

Zig followed her obediently to the bathroom. I could hear them laughing and chatting in the most exasperatingly friendly and natural way.

My father came in from the garden.

'What's going on?'

'Mummy's shaving Zig in the bathroom . . . with your razor,' I added.

'What, that fellow back again?' My father laughed indulgently. 'What does he want?'

'He wants to take me out to the cinema, but . . .' I started.

At this point Zig returned, shaven, his hair brushed and wearing a clean sweater of my father's.

'Hallo, Zig,' said my father, shaking him warmly by the hand. 'You and Julia off out are you?'

Zig said 'Yes' and I said 'No' at precisely the same time.

My father studied the sweater with a fleeting air of recognition.

'Well, don't let me keep you. You young things

want to be out enjoying yourselves, I dare say.' And he walked over to the television and turned on the news.

My father hated to be disturbed while the news was on.

So we went to the cinema.

We went to a cinema on the far side of town. It was one I had never visited before, in the Italian quarter. It took ages going by bus and by the time we arrived the programme had already started. The film they were showing was *La Dolce Vita*.

Outside the cinema I insisted that we should go Dutch.

'Oh, I thought you were going to pay for me,' said Zig. He felt in his pocket and drew out a few coins. 'Tell you what, I'll treat you to popcorn.'

'You are impossible!' I said. 'What if I had come out without any money.'

'You wouldn't do that,' said Zig. 'Girls like you always bring enough money so that you can take a taxi home if need be. You know, if I get too fresh or anything.'

It was a small, oppressively stuffy cinema. In the darkness I could sense that the auditorium was packed. The air was thick with the smell and feel of people. It was quite unlike any cinema audience I had come across before. It was a seething living mass that responded to the film with whistles and laughter and applause as if the actors could appreciate its reactions. And then I noticed the other odd thing. The film was in Italian with no subtitles.

'Do you speak Italian?' I hissed to Zig.

'No, do you?'

'No.'

'Typical,' I thought.

Zig didn't 'get fresh'. He just slouched down in his

35

seat and ate the popcorn as if it were the only meal he had had that day. Which it probably was.

When at last the lights went up I found that not only was I the sole non-Italian in the house, apart from Zig that is, I was the only female.

I felt uncomfortable as inquisitive male eyes ran over me. But Zig didn't appear to notice. Standing a good eight inches taller than the majority of the audience, he just elbowed his way through the crowd leaving me to follow as best I could.

As we entered the crush of the foyer I slipped my arm through his.

'Zig,' I said. 'Wait for me.'

When we got out into the street and the crowd began to disperse, I tried to draw my arm away.

'Don't do that,' he said.

'Do what?'

'Don't take your arm away.'

'Why not?'

'You make me feel protective.'

'You could have felt a bit more protective back there, where all those wildly randy-looking Italians were.'

'They wouldn't do you any harm. Not in a crowd like that. Probably all family men who go to mass three times on Sunday.'

'Where were their wives then?'

'Back home where they belong.'

But I didn't want to be seen walking arm in arm with Zig, so I took my arm away all the same.

He leaned over and tore a rose off a bush growing in one of the neat gardens that bordered the road. He studied it for a moment, smelt it and then thrust it through his buttonhole.

'What did you think of it?' he asked.

'The film?' I tried to think of some intelligent

36

comment. I had hardly understood anything I had seen.

'No, the experience. The experience of being part of an audience which still lives and breathes and participates in what it's being shown. None of that dry old critical crap that I dare say you've been splurging over that precious exam paper of yours all afternoon.'

I didn't say anything. Somewhere inside I felt a taut string of anxiety loosen. That dry old critical crap wasn't that vital. The English exam shrank to its correct proportions.

We caught the ten-ten bus out of town. We sat right at the back of the bus, and as I stared out of the window I started to wonder what would happen when Zig took me home. I started to think about what I would do, if no . . . when, he tried to kiss me, because I didn't want him to. It wouldn't have mattered if it had just been another of the Australian boys I'd met, because I probably would have just let them and thought no more about it. But I liked Zig. How did you explain that to a boy for goodness' sake?

But I didn't have to think about it for long, because Zig suddenly got to his feet and said:

'Hey. Here's my stop,' and went headlong down the bus just leaving me sitting there.

As I looked out of the window I saw him standing by the road and waving. He tried to throw something through the top part of the window which was open. I think it was the rose but I couldn't be sure because a car behind us ran over it.

So I paid for my fare and Zig's fare and walked home from the bus stop alone.

'Where's Zig?' asked my mother when I came into the sitting-room. 'Didn't he bring you home?'

'Oh, he had to get back. I think he had an essay to

finish or something.' Why was I telling white lies to defend him?

'Oh, dear,' she said. 'Oh, well, I suppose I can wash it as well now.' She was sitting mending Zig's sweater.

'But I do hope he'll bring your father's back, it was quite new.' she added.

'What's that, dear?' said my father.

Chapter Four

Zig: Bragge was whopping ketchup on his double curry, rice and chips. He had worked out that, penny for penny, you could get the biggest gut-fill on the double curry, and since ketchup came free he wasn't going to miss out.

Bragge was trying to put on body weight and this could be expensive. I selected a beef salad. I didn't give a damn about this Australian body ethic. Bragge, on the other hand, thought more muscle might help him on the women scene but frankly, as I told him, they either find you riveting or they don't.

I joined him. The refectory was sweltering. I could see sweat running down Bragge's face as the combined forces of heat inside him from the hot spicy food and heat outside in the room bombarded his body system. Honestly, you could see why females didn't go for him.

'You owe me five quid,' I said.

Bragge eyed me, chewing slowly.

'No, I don't.'

'Yep. That bet we made last week.'

'What bet?'

I could see it. Bragge was going to have one of his memory failures. And I needed that fiver.

'The ice-maiden.'

'Come off it.'

'Nope. Got a date with her on Tuesday.'

'I don't believe it.'

'That's why I need the fiver.'

Bragge filled his mouth with grease-oozing chips and eyed me as he chewed.

'She wouldn't walk to the end of the street with you.'

'Wanna bet?'

'I don't believe you.'

'Look Bragge, do I ever have you on?'

'Yes.'

'Come on, I need that fiver or all that effort's wasted.'

''Spose she's really got the hots for you,' said Bragge, with quite unnecessary sarcasm.

'She's mildly interested.'

'Mildly interested. Come on, you can do better than that.'

'Invited me in for a meal up at her place.' I deliberately edited out the parent bit. Well, Bragge wasn't interested in her parents, was he?

'Champagne and caviar?'

'Lamb chops, actually.'

'Sounds romantic.'

'Look, Bragge. I'm telling you the honest truth.'

'OK prove it.'

'OK. I'm taking her out to the flicks on Tuesday. You can come along and see for yourself.'

'Me come along with you and your bird? I've got better things to do.'

'OK, so let me have the fiver then.'

'Which cinema you going to?'

'Thought I'd take her to the Italian place.'

'You'll have to walk back down Neal Street.'

'Yep.'

'OK. If I see you walk back down there, ice-maiden in tow, you get the fiver.'

'Swear it?'

'Yep.'

It was the best I could do. Next thing I had to work out was how to borrow a fiver off her for the tickets. Still a girl like that must be loaded. That wouldn't be a problem.

It wasn't surprising Bragge didn't believe me. It was pretty bloody incredible. She was such an odd girl. She had arrived at the University out of the blue. A nice little English girl driven down in a brand new ice-blue Jaguar by one of those silver-haired Englishmen who look like they've stepped out of a whisky advert. She was a joke. That's why Bragge had had a bet with me.

The thing started one lunchtime. Bragge and I were stretched out on the campus lawn watching the talent eating its lunch and having one of those Braggish sort of discussions about why he never scored. I was kind of trying to reassure him that it wasn't to do with money, or his clothes, or his lack of muscle weight, without telling the poor sod the cruel truth that it was really his total lack of sex-appeal, which, when you come to think of it, is pretty well incurable.

Anyway, that's when I came up with this theory that it was all technique. Bragge was getting really interested because if it was technique, it was something he might possibly be able to learn, so there was actually hope for him on this earth.

'You mean, with the right technique, you think you could pretty well pull any girl?'

'Sure,' I said, just to kind of ease his pain and suffering.

'Bet you couldn't that one,' he said.

And I looked over and saw this dark-haired specimen I'd kind of noticed before, getting into that icy-coloured car with that incredibly aloof sort of expression of hers.

'No problem,' I said.

'Bet you anything you couldn't.'

'A fiver?'

'Sure.'

So I was kind of committed. It wasn't just the money, I had to prove to Bragge the technique theory, poor sod.

Anyway, it was a challenge and anything was better than mooning around over my own state of affairs. So I took the whole thing seriously. I observed her movements for a few days and found out the basic facts: origin, name, faculty. It wasn't difficult; whoever you see in a town like this is bound to be known by someone you meet.

The surprise was that when I came in and tackled her, she didn't just tell me to piss off. At least not right away. Not the way the native females would. She looked at me in that aloof manner of hers as if she was suspending judgment. And then her parents! Things got curiouser and curiouser. They actually seemed to like me. And I liked them and that was really disconcerting. I mean, I'd entered into this as a purely financial transaction with Bragge. I didn't want to get involved.

After that first meeting, I left it for a few days just so that she would get to kind of wonder why I didn't phone her or anything. Then I realised I hadn't got her damn number. They were in a rented house and everything, so I couldn't look it up in the book. Do you know, I hung around the campus for three days and that girl didn't show up. It was the hardest fiver I've ever earned.

So there was nothing for it but to hoof it all the way up to Floreat Park and collar her at home.

When I arrived, what did I find in the garden? A baby screaming blue murder, not a sign of anyone. So I picked the child up before it could have convulsions or anything and she came flying out of the house as if I was about to make off with it. Come to think of it, that was really ironic.

'Would you like some tea or something?' she asked when we had got the baby back to sleep.

The breeze was swishing through the willow trees in the garden and I was lying back in the old wicker rocker of theirs watching her, and I decided I quite liked how her hair hung in a tangled sort of way like the willow trees swishing in the breeze.

No, I didn't want tea, but with the quietness and the soft swish of the willows, I wondered for just a moment about the 'or something'.

So I just rocked and watched her. She didn't say anything for quite a while. I expect she was waiting for me to make the first move. But I was in no hurry.

Then she started to talk about the work she had to do. If

42

there's one thing I can't stand it's women going on about their work. So I decided it was about time to go, anyway. I didn't get round to asking her out till I was actually outside the gate. Then she came out with all this garbage about this guy she'd been dating before me. I mean, as if I cared! I'd only asked her out to the flicks after all. So I made a couple of discreet enquiries about just how thick she was with this creep and then she really got mad.

She said I got on her nerves. I took it as a good sign. I was obviously getting through to her.

That's when I got down to my dissertation. Well, it was the least I could do. It had obviously started to bother Selwyn – he's my tutor – although I kept on reassuring him how well it was going. And it *was* going well in a way, although I hadn't actually written any of it down. So I decided to give Selwyn a break because he was a good guy, and although it was only a week overdue, I felt perhaps I was almost building up enough of a feeling of urgency to commit some of my thoughts to paper.

Then suddenly, right in the middle of the first set of conclusions, it was Tuesday. In spite of throwing up the chance of finishing what was perhaps one of the most definitive things written maybe since Wittgenstein, I actually decided I couldn't let the girl down, so I just dropped everything and took a bus up to her place.

Daphne seemed a bit surprised to see me, but I don't expect Julia tells her everything she's up to. Julia was in the bathroom and she took some time dolling herself up for me, hairwashing etc.

Daphne fussed about me shaving and she made me shave with Henry's razor. It was a bit of a job because in her enthusiasm she had put in two blades.

She made me wear Henry's dreadful tasteless sweater as well.

In the bus Julia said, 'I didn't think you'd come tonight.'
'Why not?'

'Because of the row we had.'

'What row?'

'You know, the row we had about what you asked me when you left.'

'What was that?'

'You must remember.'

I couldn't for the life of me remember anything except she'd been all funny and prudish about her blasted boyfriend.

'Oh about *him*.'

'Exactly.'

'He tends to crop up a lot in conversation, doesn't he?'

'Does he?'

'Yes, he does as a matter of fact. Does he have to come with us everywhere we go?'

She laughed. 'No, of course not.'

I think I handled the ticket-buying quite well. I had been worrying about the logistics of the money business on the bus and wishing that I had managed to extricate the five quid from Bragge. But there was no need. As it happened, I was just about to ask her if she could lend me some cash when she offered to pay, for herself at any rate. In the end she paid for me as well and I splashed out on some popcorn.

During the film I got sort of conscious of her bare shoulder next to mine. I think she probably expected me to put my arm round the back of her seat and get interested. But, frankly, I wasn't going to give her the satisfaction. This must have got through to her because on the way out she slipped her arm through mine in a really possessive female sort of way.

I liked the feel of her arm. She had good girlish slim wrists, and then suddenly I remembered Bragge and I knew that just round the next corner we were going to be passing his place, and with any luck I was going to get the fiver and I hadn't even had to fork out for the cinema seats.

When we got level with his house I paused for a moment

and tore a rose off this great corny rose bush he had growing in his garden. I waited just long enough under a streetlight to make sure that he could really get a good look at us. That is, assuming the bastard was looking out of his window.

I felt really good all the way to the bus stop. I felt almost like I used to before Su-Yen. And this buoyant mood must have rubbed off on Julia because we talked about the film and I could feel her kind of loosening up inside that tight British shell of hers.

Then she said some really dumb things about Australia, you know the way the British do, in an old imperialist kind of way, which I pointed out and she laughed. In fact, I was feeling really good about her and I was even considering giving the girl a break and asking her out again.

We caught the ten-ten bus out of town. She walked up right to the back of the bus and, following her up, I suddenly got this overpowering insight into how she really did remind me of Su-Yen. It was something about the way she walked and all that dark hair.

Then I knew that if I took her home I was going to get into all that physical scene and 'when were we going to see each other again?' And I knew at the moment, just now, I couldn't cope with all that. Not yet anyway. Not so soon.

Chapter Five

Julia: Luckily the weather turned rather warmer and my father didn't notice that his new sweater was not in the drawer. A week or so went by and there was no sign of Zig. His sweater lay neatly darned and washed in the clothes basket, and each time I passed it I felt a sharp pang of annoyance that somewhere he was swanning around in a new blue pure wool English Lyle and Scott.

I didn't have so much work for a while and between lectures I took to idling in the campus Coffee Shop.

You could starve stylishly in the Coffee Shop. You could get an open sandwich with about two strands of tinned asparagus on top for the same as a price of a meal in the Refectory. Australians always go on about just what an incredibly un-snobbish country they live in. It's a load of rot. They actually create their own social divisions. The Coffee Shop/Refectory divide was the campus one. People who starved in the Coffee Shop didn't mix with people who ate in the Refectory.

It was in the Coffee Shop that, perched elegantly on a stool surrounded by a deliciously foreign haze of French cigarette smoke, I came across Anthony.

'Darling, come and give me a kiss. Aren't you looking divine and why aren't you wearing that yummy perfume you know I love?'

'If I'd known you were coming I would have put it on specially for you. What are you doing here?'

46

Anthony was a friend from Paul's year, so had already graduated. When at the University, he had surrounded himself with a small élite coterie of friends who had earned themselves a title which delighted him: 'The Degenerates'. They gave, in Anthony's phrase, 'the most divine parties.'

'Now, Julia, what's all this I've been hearing about you?'

'What have you been hearing about me?' I asked, amused.

'About this "person" you've been seen with?'

'What "person"?' I asked defensively.

'Well, of course, it's absolutely nothing to do with me. But I did hear that you were seen around with someone who didn't sound your type at all.'

'What *is* my type?'

'I thought Paul was.'

'He is, but that doesn't mean to say that I can't even speak to anyone else. It's not as if we were engaged or anything.'

'But I was given to believe you *were*, practically.'

'There's a lot of difference between being "practically" engaged to someone who is a couple of thousand miles away and totally owned. I've got to get out sometimes, you know.'

'But honestly, darling, if you're bored, you could always come over and see me.'

'All right, I will,' I said, glad that the conversation had turned away from Zig. I liked Anthony and it was difficult to reconcile my affection for him and the total antipathy I knew he would have for Zig.

Through Anthony's eyes I could see Zig's appalling lack of charisma. I suddenly imagined him walking into the Coffee Room unshaven, in his dirty sneakers and still wearing my father's best blue sweater.

Unlikely as it seemed, the very thought made me hurriedly gather my books.

'Look I'm sorry, I've got a lecture to get to.'

'What a conscientious person you are. Nobody, but nobody, goes to lectures, you know. It's just not done.'

'I do,' I said.

'Well, next time that gorgeous Paul rings you, give him a big kiss from me, won't you.'

'I'm not sure if he'd like that.'

'I knew him first, you know,' said Anthony and he blew a perfect smoke-ring.

'Voilà, un disque bleu,' he said contentedly.

Of course, Anthony was right, Zig was impossible, a joke. I told myself firmly that once I had sorted out this sweater business, that would be the end of it. I would not see Zig again.

I didn't go to the lecture. I walked down the sandy track that led to Cormorant Point. I had found a small dry cove on the riverside which was sheltered from the wind and from time to time I used to go down there instead of to the libary to read. I opened my book and the sun shone down enclosing me in its warmth. It glittered enticingly on the swiftly alternating wavelets that swept across the bay. I thought of what Anthony had said about me and Paul. And I pushed from my mind any grey intangible doubt that might be lurking there and allowed myself to bask in a warm secure feeling of certainty that all was as it should be in the best of all possible worlds.

I must have been there for about an hour. At the end of that time I had decided precisely what I must do. I had been carrying Zig's old sweater about with me for days in the expectation of bumping into him on the campus. I now made my way across to the Philosophy Department.

I didn't want to risk going into a tutor's study so I

hovered for a while in the gloomy corridor, hoping that someone would come by and direct me to the Common Room. No one did. At length, by a process of elimination, I worked my way down to a door which bore no message but from behind which emanated a series of thumps and laughs.

I gingerly opened the door, to find a missile hurled across the room narrowly missed me.

'Out!' exclaimed a voice.

'No, that's not fair, the wicket moved.'

'Come in, will you, and close the wicket,' commanded a voice.

'Do you want to join in? Do you play sock cricket?' The boy picked up the rolled-up ball of socks and held them out to me by way of explanation. 'We could do with a fielder if you're any good.'

I explained who I was looking for.

'Oh Zarathustra! Not been seen around these parts for days. Gone to earth, writing the definitive answer to the meaning of life.'

'Where can I find him them?'

'Stand back. Can't you see I'm trying to bowl?' I moved out of the line of fire directed at the wicket chalked on the door.

'You could try his home.'

So I did.

Sinclair Street looked more run-down than ever in the low afternoon sunlight. I didn't know which number he lived at, so chose the most encouraging looking house and rang the bell.

After a pause, a young woman with a small child hanging on to her skirt opened the door. She eyed me suspiciously.

'Yes?'

'I'm sorry to bother you, but could you tell me where the Zuchelskis live?'

'The who?'

49

'The Zuchelskis. They're Polish.'

'Oh them.' She looked at me inquisitively. 'Number seventeen.'

Number seventeen was one of the poorer houses in the street but, unlike the others, the front garden had a neat flower bed set before the house in which bloomed a single row of tulips.

I tried to imagine Zig planting those tulips but it seemed improbable.

I hesitated before ringing the bell. Suddenly I felt embarrassed, wondering if I would meet Zig's grandmother and what reception I would get. The net curtains of the house across the road twitched and I could feel I was being watched.

I rang. After a moment the door opened and Zig stood there staring at me.

He looked dreadful.

'What are you doing here?' he asked.

'Well, that's a great welcome. Aren't you going to ask me in?' I could feel the scrutiny of the neighbours over the road.

'No, you can't come in.'

'Why ever not?'

'The place is in a mess.'

'Oh, don't be ridiculous. I don't care even if it is.'

There was a call from inside. An elderly woman's voice speaking a language I presumed to be Polish. Zig answered her. The gentle flowing line of the language sounded strange on his lips.

'There, I can hear your grandmother is asking who it is. I'd like to meet her.'

'No, you can't come in.' His hand shook as he held the door ajar. 'You see, she wouldn't like it if the place wasn't tidy. It would hurt her pride if I asked you in.'

'I've brought your sweater.' I took it out of my bag and handed it to him.

'Thanks.' He took it and was about to shut the door.

'Zig, haven't you forgotten something?'

'What?'

'You've still got my father's brand new blue sweater.'

'OK, you wait there, I'll get it.'

He shut the door in my face. I had to linger on the path in full view of the net curtains opposite.

The door opened just wide enough to allow the sweater through.

'Are you all right, Zig?'

'Sure, I've been working that's all. Haven't had much sleep. Got to get back to it actually.'

I could hear from his voice that he was really keen to get rid of me. So I left and all the way back home I thought how curiously he had behaved. Not like Zig at all.

And so for a while I literally forgot about Zig. And I presumed he forgot about me. My friends and his friends, assuming he had any, moved in different circles and so our paths never crossed.

The weather was growing hotter and when the wind blew from the East you felt the hot breath of the Nullarbor Plain, forerunner of the summer to come. It was a dry wind, almost imperceptibly scented with the face-powder smell of red bush dust. Day by day the sky was assuming that dome of uninterrupted blue that each year spanned the days from October through to March.

The pace seemed to slacken. Heat haze lingered in the campus gardens, where the rotary hoses lazily swung their great arcs of water over the scarlet and green canna lillies.

I settled into a relaxed pattern of University life. I went to lectures, filled pages with notes, dutifully handed in essays. At weekends I generally went to the beach with Glen, the lazy-voiced American girl. We would lie stretched out, comparing the relative merits of the boys who passed, and from time to time Glen would describe, in more detail than I found absolutely necessary, what she had done with her boyfriend the night before.

I auditioned for a part in the first year Drama Society production, forgetting as usual my proneness to stage fright in the enthusiasm of the moment. Flattered to be selected for quite a large part, I only discovered later it was not so much on the strength of my acting ability as on account of my English vowels. The play was *The Importance of Being Earnest*.

Apart from rehearsals I spent any other free time at Anthony's.

'Come in, darling I'm always "At Home".' And everyone did, much to the dismay of his German landlord, of whom Anthony did a perfect impersonation.

Lodging a nailbrush between his nose and upper lip he would proclaim: 'Vot is all dis here? Zis is a private house. Not zo much noise or I get ze pleece.'

Then Anthony would turn up his favourite Marlene Dietrich record and join in, savouring the part where she sings: 'Men flutter round me like motts around a flame . . .'

And we would drink anything anyone happened to have brought along and listen to Barry Humphries records until the air was blue with Disque Bleu smoke and Anthony would suggest going to CJ's.

CJ's was a Greek restaurant and bar with a late licence, but somehow we had managed to turn it into a nightclub. We danced to Chuck Berry and the Beach Boys and prided ourselves on having introduced the 'Twist' into Australia.

Too late, I would usually remember that I was due home and there would be a mad rush for a cab.

It was after one of these evenings that I was 'gated'. I quietly unlatched the door to find my mother, a tower of indignation in housecoat and hairnet, standing in the hall.

There was a lot of 'Where have you been?', and 'What time do you think this is?', and 'Those dreadful people you know' and 'Totally unsuitable'. And the end-result was the clamp-down on funds so that in the evenings I was confined to the house.

The fact that this coincided with my getting a failure mark in a philosophy assessment didn't help matters. I paced the house like a caged lion. I was finding it difficult to study and everything seemed to be going from bad to worse.

Chapter Six

Zig: I really blew it with that girl. She caught me off guard. Coming to the house like that without warning. I should have let her in right there and then. At least we would have known where we stood.

I hesitated for a moment and considered whether I could quite face the whole business of her going into that side of things. While I was considering, she kind of scrabbled around in her bag and then she yanked out a sweater, my sweater. And I could tell from the final kind of way she handed it over that this was the brush-off. So why the hell was I even considering involving her in the whole goddam story.

I made up some really puny excuse about my grandmother minding her coming in and because we'd been speaking Polish the words that came out sounded kind of strange.

So I took the sweater and I could see it had been washed and darned really nicely and for a moment I could see Julia with my sweater full of my body-vibes on her lap, mending it, and I hoped it gave her a thrill in a possessive female sort of way to stitch it up.

'Haven't you forgotten something?'

For a moment I thought . . . she knows. She must know the whole goddam story, everyone must. But it seemed that all she wanted was to get back Henry's tasteless blue sweater.

Julia giving me the push like that made me feel pretty low. It even sort of permeated the work I was trying to do. A good week later these mean kind of twinges of bad feeling were still creeping up on me right in the middle of a sentence. I've got pretty wonderful concentration, so when that happens I take notice. In fact, I was feeling so low that I knew I was pretty well scraping along the bottom. I just couldn't get any lower.

That's when I re-read my dissertation. It was the biggest load of self-righteous crap I had ever read. I was about half-way through the third page when my grandmother shouted that the hot water boiler had gone out again. So I took the whole lot into the kitchen and screwed it up page by page into neat symmetrical balls, piled these up in the ashes and made an ingenious superstructure of kindling over it. It burned better than newspaper. Probably all the size in the paper or something. In fact for once I didn't have to rake it all out and start again. The boiler lit first time and I felt really fine as it burned.

'That's good,' said my grandmother and she screwed up her face the way she always did when she was pleased.

I watched the flames with satisfaction. It was a 'good' blaze.

Once the boiler was well and truly lit, I walked out of the house. I usually walk when I feel vile. It's one of those non-activities you can kind of wear yourself out doing with the minimum of effort. I didn't care too much where I walked and I soon found myself in the city. It was late shopping night and although it was getting dark in the street, it was still light under the arcades. I slowed down for a time listening to the ingratiating voices of the store advertisements being broadcast over their loudspeaker systems. As I made my way along the street between the neon-lit faces of the late shoppers, the voices vied with each other for attention.

'And a special offer for this week only, fully sanforised' .... 'at prices you can't resist' ... 'Come and try our imported underwear ladies ...' I couldn't get over the imported underwear girl's voice, she had this really prim kind of way of saying, 'Wired under-cup bra.' It just killed me the way the 'p' and the 'b' came together with a kind of lip-smacking lisp. I had to stop for a while to hear it round again.

I was just standing there listening like some pervert or something, while she was droning through all the boring 'Nylon hosiery in sixteen fashion shades', business, when this poster caught my eye. Someone had fly-posted this handbill up on a lamppost. It kind of went round the sides so you couldn't see it all at once. But I could read the middle.

sity Drama Socie

presents
MPORTAN–
F BEIN
EARNEST

And under that, in among the smaller letters, 'Cily Cardew: Julia Summerv'.

I craned around the lamppost to read what it said. It was Julia's name all right. It seemed she was acting in some creepy first year drama production. Boy, how I hated all those Dram. Soc. types, all 'darling this' and 'weren't-you-wonderful'. Most of them put on a better act off-stage than on it. Trust Julia to get mixed up in a scene like that.

I checked the dates. This was the last night. Well, maybe I ought to go and do the girl a favour and look in, probably only be a measly handful of people in the audience anyway.

The play was well under way when I arrived at the Dram. Soc. Theatre, which was quite lucky because I just walked in at the back without having to fork out for a ticket or anything. The theatre was pretty packed actually. I think the play must have been on the English Syllabus or something.

I was just easing myself along a row into a seat that was going begging – honestly, people can be inconsiderate when you're trying to negotiate yourself over their feet and bags and goddam coats and everything – when I heard Julia's voice:

'May I offer you some tea, Miss Fairfax?'

And for a moment I thought I heard the creak of the old wicker rocker and the breeze swishing through the willow trees.

But the Julia on stage was not the Julia I knew, with her hair hanging loose and tangled. Her hair was tightly tied back and she was wearing a stiff high-necked white dress.

'Sugar?' she said, with too much emphasis.

I watched intrigued by this strange metamorphosis. It was like watching Julia over-acting Julia.

'Cake or bread and butter?' she demanded.

The other girl replied: 'Bread and butter, please. Cake is rarely seen at the best houses nowadays.'

The other girl was having a little trouble with her English accent, but she was a far better actress.

I watched Julia's face while this girl was going barmy about cake and bread and butter and how many lumps of sugar there were in her tea; and I suddenly became aware of what an enormous gulf separated us. I mean we had nothing, but absolutely nothing in common.

She got to her feet: 'To save my poor, innocent, trusting boy from the machinations of any other girl there are no lengths to which I would not go.'

Boy she was overacting. But she really had a pretty good body in that close-fitting dress. I mean, I expect the tight belt was pulling her in at the waist a good bit, but she didn't have a bad body. The stage does that to people, they only have to get up on those goddam boards with everyone kind of ogling them and you suddenly think they look pretty good. I guess that's why they go through all the pain and agony of learning all those lines and dying of stage fright and everything.

I was starting to wonder who this 'Earnest' creep was anyway? I didn't have long to wait. They seemed pretty thick those two. All that putting his arm around her waist and kissing and stuff. I started to wonder how many rehearsals there had been. I mean, maybe he was her type.

57

Some ego-tripping Dram. Soc. freak could well be the kind of guy Julia went for. And there would be one of those dreadful end of play Dram. Soc. parties later tonight, with everyone oozing smoothie congratulations at each other. God the whole thing made me sick. It made me so sick that I decided I was going to have to get out of there or I might just throw up or something. So I started to climb back over all those people in my row. What a fuss they made! You would have thought that we were in the goddam Opera House or something. I mean if they hadn't shushed so loud I don't think Julia would have even noticed that I'd been to see her in her beastly play.

It was pretty awful when she missed that cue though. I felt bad about that. At last she heard the prompt.

'It's not a very pleasant position for a young girl suddenly to find herself in. Is it?' was the line I heard her say as I made it into the foyer.

I felt better when I got outside. I walked along the river front and there was a bit of a breeze blowing in my face. The lights from the Causeway were reflecting long and deep across the ink-black river. I thought for a bit about Su. All this Julia business was pretty insignificant really. She was just a nice little prim English girl. I didn't want to get mixed up in a scene like that. I wished she'd go back where she belonged. I wished she'd go back to her precious green lawns and tea cups and English public school boys. What the hell was she doing over here anyway?

I started throwing stones in the river. There were lots of pretty decent flat stones so I started fooling around playing ducks and drakes. I didn't beat my record, but I got a stone to bounce six times, which was enough, so I turned back inland.

I didn't sleep too well that night. I kept wondering if that 'Earnest' creep had taken her home. Well, what was it to me anyway?

* * *

The next day I started my dissertation again.

It took about ten days, more or less. I lost count of time. When I had finished, I actually managed to read it through without puking. I'd taught myself to type in a sort of clumsy four finger manner. It took time, but it saved money. Once typed, I read it through again. It looked like someone else's work, and full of someone else's fallacies. But at any rate, it was done. Having tracked down a piece of brown paper, I made it into a neat tight parcel which I tied with string. I wrote on the front, Mr S. Selwyn. Then I thought that looked too damn formal, so I crossed it out and wrote 'Selwyn'.

The angle of the sun through my window told me it must be about five-ish. I wasn't going to trust my life's work to the vagaries of the Post Office. I could hear grandma humming in the kitchen, so it was all right to go out. I picked up the parcel and walked out of the house.

There was a finality about handing in the parcel. Once out of my hands it would be perused in all its nakedness, vulnerable to coffee cups, and fumbling fingers and mad paper-chewing dogs. I tried to remember, did Selwyn have a dog?

I was feeling kind of sick in the stomach at the thought of handing it over. I wanted to see it get right into Selwyn's hands. It would be one of those moments you would remember. I made a mental note to record exactly what he said as he took it.

'You can leave it in his in-tray if you like, but he won't be in for a couple of days.'

Selwyn's secretary blew on her newly-varnished nails and eyed me with a professional's disdain for undergraduates.

'What do you mean, he's not here? Where's he gone?'

'He's gone to Bunbury, fishing for a few days. Back on Monday, but as I said, you can leave it if you like. It'll be quite safe. After all, it's not much use to anyone else, is it?'

Did the woman realise that she was talking about the most revolutionary piece of writing to come out of the Twentieth Century?

I placed it reverently in the in-tray and stood staring at it. The full significance of Selwyn's absence sank in. This meant, of course, that if I wanted, I could have two whole days to revise it.

What the hell.

The Common Room welcomed me with its familiar stale breath smell. I moved a couple of half-full coffee cups off the decaying sofa and sat down.

'Finished it?' someone enquired without much interest.'

'Yeah, s'pose so, in as much as it'll ever be finished.'

'Hey, there was some female came in for you.'

'Who?'

'Didn't give a name.'

'What did she look like?'

Leon screwed up his eyes thoughtfully. 'Long dark hair. Good legs, not much tit.'

So Su-Yen had finally come round.

'When?'

''Bout a week ago.'

'Thanks.'

I was at the door.

'Hey, want to come to a party tonight? You could bring her along.' Leon was always trying to get his hands on other guys' girls.

It seemed someone he and Bragge vaguely knew was giving a party. I scrawled down the address and left.

Su-Yen lived downtown in the Italian sector. The rents were low down there and her hostessing didn't bring in much considering.

I made my way up the concrete stairway with its familiar old smell of cats. The kids in the first floor flat were screaming as usual, probably trying to make themselves heard over the din of the television.

I paused at her door to look back out over the city where the first lights were already winking in the warm evening air. I took a deep breath and made a conscious effort to look relaxed.

I pressed the door-bell and heard it ring somewhere deep inside the flat. Of course, it was highly likely that she would be out.

'Who is it?' Su's voice came from the other side of the door.

'Me.'

There was a moment's silence and then a scrabbling with the chain.

Su's face appeared round the door. It wasn't right that a girl like her should look so goddam perfect.

'What you want?'

'I want to talk to you.'

'OK, talk. I'm listening.'

'Not here,' I pushed the door a bit. I could just see that she was wearing that thin silky thing of hers and that she didn't have much, if anything, underneath.

'I didn't say you could come in.'

'Look, for God's sake, Su. They said you came down to see me last week.'

'Who said?'

'The guys. You know, Bragge and that lot. They said you came looking for me in the Common Room.'

'Me looking for you. That's rich,' and she started to laugh. She laughed in an ugly mocking way straight in my face and that made me really mad.

I took a step back and I just went for that door with full force and it flew open. She wasn't strong enough to hold it back, I knew she wouldn't be. And for a moment I was standing there in her hall, getting my breath back and staring at her, when this guy came out of the bedroom.

I don't remember walking down the stairs, or how I crossed the city, but I must have, because the next thing I was conscious of was standing in this off-licence somewhere near the city centre. For once I had some money in my pocket. I bought some beers with Bragge's five pounds and I drank four straight off till the pain started to recede a bit. He hadn't hit me or anything. There was no need. I'm a conscientious objector when it comes to fights. I just backed out. It would have been a waste of his effort hitting me anyway, I wouldn't have felt it. I was hurting too much already, inside.

When I'd got a few beers down, somehow I must have found my way up to Floreat Park. I took Julia to that party instead.

She was pretty Julia-ish all evening but it was a comfort in a way to have something female beside me, salve on wounded pride I guess.

She disappeared sometime during the evening and I think I got pretty disgustingly drunk. Which, come to think of it, is probably why she disappeared.

I woke up the next day with the most almighty hangover and for once I remembered what I had dreamt.

Su was sitting in the Common Room dressed in that flimsy silk thing. It was night-time but all the guys were there, Bragge and Leon and everyone. She had my sweater on her lap and she was unpicking the darning.

'You've got to marry me, Su,' I was saying. 'You've got to now.'

But she just smiled that secret smile of hers and said: 'Not till I've finished this darning.'

'But you're undoing it Su,' I kept saying.

And she laughed that open-mouthed mocking laugh that made me feel like I was nothing. Worse than nothing. Then Bragge and Leon and the other guys started laughing as well, and I reached down and put my hand over Su's mouth to close that gaping hole of a laughing mouth and when I looked down I saw it wasn't her at all, it was Julia.

I lay there for a long time trying to figure out the dream.

Chapter Seven

Julia: It was Friday evening, my parents were out having dinner with friends, and the door bell rang.

I peered through the mosquito mesh into the dark outside.

'Who is it?'

'Me.'

'Zig!' I was really pleased to see him and it must have shown in my voice.

He had made a real effort for Zig. He had shaved and he was actually wearing shoes instead of dirty sneakers. Black leather shoes that were rather dated, but they were shoes.

He hovered in the hall. He was carrying a brown paper bag under his arm and he shifted it from one side to the other.

'Come in. Come and sit down. What have you been up to?'

'Where are your parents?'

'Out.'

'You on your own?' He looked around briefly. 'When will they be back?'

'I'm not sure. They've gone out to dinner.'

Zig stretched out on the sofa, delved into the paper bag and brought out a can of beer. He snapped off the ring pull and was about to drink, then hesitated.

'Want some?' he said, offering me the can.

'No thanks, I don't like beer.' I got him a glass.

As he poured in the beer I noticed again how his hand shook.

'Zig, are you all right?' I asked. 'How much have you been drinking tonight?'

He settled himself more comfortably on to the sofa: 'Never been better. I finished my dissertation, you know.'

'What's it about?'

'Right, wrong and responsibility.'

'I'm thinking of giving up philosophy,' I said. 'I got an F for my last assessment essay.'

'Most people are pretty hopeless to start with,' he said. 'It's one of those things you get better at the more you do it. Like sex, you know,' he said.

'No, actually, I don't know,' I said huffily.

'Oh, sorry if I embarrassed you. That was embarrassment, wasn't it?'

'Look, Zig. What do you want? Why have you come? If it's to irritate me you can just go.'

'Actually, I came to ask you out to a party.'

'Oh,' I said non-committally. I hadn't been to a party for ages, not since the Dram. Soc. one, which reminded me . . .

'But since your parents are out, why bother? We could just as easily stay here and maybe I could give you a hand with what we were talking about earlier.'

'What?'

'Philosophy, of course,' he glanced at me out of his half-closed slavic eyes. It was a look without a hint of irony. A perfect poker player's look.

'Why on earth should you waste your time on me?'

'Nothing better to do. Not at the moment at any rate.'

'You could go to the party.'

'Too early.'

'Zig, you know I only ever . . .' I hesitated. 'I only want to be friends.'

'Do you think I'm totally insensitive?'

I thought for a moment. In fact, I suddenly realised

that he was one of the most sensitive people I have ever met. I didn't know how, I just knew it.

So I changed the subject.

'By the way, thanks a lot for your "guest appearance" at the Dram. Soc. Play.'

'Oh, did you think I was good?' he asked.

'Brilliant. Quite stole the show. Specially the way you tripped over the bottom step on the way out.'

'Sorry about that.' He looked really apologetic.

'Doesn't matter really. Actually I was killing myself. I couldn't say a word in case I shrieked with laughter. It was that great pompous idiot who was playing Algernon who was furious. You ruined one of his favourite lines.'

'Oh, I hope I didn't spoil a beautiful relationship between you two,' he said, giving me the tiniest sidelong look.

'You must be joking,' I replied.

Zig said nothing. He just took another can out of his brown paper bag and, snapping off the pull, drank from it.

We were silent for a few mintues.

'What's the problem anyway?' he asked after a while.

'What problem?'

'The problem with the essay?'

'Oh that! Personal identity.'

'Let's see it then.'

'It's very bad,' I said. But I was glad to relieve the tension by getting up and finding it.

Zig read it slowly with a series of grunts and he shook his head taking deep gulps of beer.

'You're right, it's hopeless.'

'I know,' I agreed ruefully.

And so Zig started to explain what I should have grasped from the lectures.

65

He had a very simple way of explaining. He stripped the whole thing down to the bare bones. And he didn't mind how idiotic the questions I asked might be. He made it all sound so obvious, explaining the story of the Philosopher's old Ford car. We took it apart and we put it back together again, piece in relation to piece. And I suddenly felt I could communicate with him in a way that was unexpected and quite different from the normal run of people I met. Somehow, it was curiously hypnotic.

And then the phone rang.

The sound cut accusingly into the room and I knew it was Paul ringing.

'Aren't you going to answer it?'

'No, I can't.'

The ringing seemed to go on and on, and then it stopped abruptly, reproachfully.

I could see Zig knew who was ringing.

'Come here,' he said, making a space for me on the sofa.

'No, I can't,' I said again.

He looked at the beer can in his hand, drank it dry, then threw it with force through the open window and we heard it clatter down the tarmac driveway.

He got up and stood looking after it with his hands in his pockets, his back to me.

'Let's go to the party then,' I suggested.

The party was on the West side of town, Zig was in a morose mood and stared out of the bus window most of the way there. I started to regret going, it was far further that I thought. I had left a note for my parents and planned to get the midnight bus back, having no money for a taxi. I hoped Zig would at least see me home.

When we got to the corner of the street we could

66

hear the noise from the party and neighbours were leaning on their gates complaining. We were just about to go in when Zig stopped in his tracks.

'Better get some more beer,' he said.

I followed him back to the off-licence, trying to persuade him that he had had quite enough to drink already.

Once back at the party we found the house was packed and had the atmosphere of a hothouse. I didn't see anyone I knew, but a few people seemed to know Zig. We started off in the kitchen where Zig leaned against the fridge talking to an incredibly tall boy in tones I couldn't hear over the noise of the music. I was getting bored and couldn't find anything to drink, so I wandered off into the room where the dancing was going on.

Couples were crammed together in a space so small that they could only manage a smoochie sort of dance. Then a strong arm grabbed me round the waist and I heard a voice in my ear saying:

'My very favourite girl. What are you doing here?'

'Julian.'

It was Paul's brother.

'What are you doing here?' I asked.

'Looking for you, of course.' He was joking.

Julian steered me into the room in a crushing embrace doing a teasing mock-romantic slow-dance.

'I've been dying to do this,' he crooned in my ear.

'Julian, stop being so silly. How's that gorgeous girlfriend of yours?'

He was just whispering in my ear an account of just how gorgeous she was, when I noticed Zig standing and watching us from the doorway.

I wriggled free from Julian as Zig made his way over to us.

'Meet Zig, he's coaching me in philosophy.' I introduced them.

But Zig ignored Julian's outstretched hand and said thickly:

'It's about time we had a dance.'

Zig held me so tight it hurt.

'You're drunk,' I said.

'So what, you don't mind if he dances like this with you.'

'Zig, don't be daft. That's Paul's brother. He was only fooling around.'

'So it's all right if it's all in the family, is it? Do they take it in turns?'

'Don't be so disgusting,' I said. 'Zig, let me go, I hate you like this, you've had too much too drink.'

He stumbled and leaned on me. 'Come outside in the garden,' he said roughly.

'Julia. I'll take you home now,' Julian was standing beside me.

'What if she doesn't want to go,' said Zig belligerently.

'But she does. Don't you, Julia,' said Julian firmly. I nodded.

I allowed Julian to lead me out of the house. I tried to say goodbye to Zig but he just turned on his heel and disappeared into the kitchen.

'Got to get a drink,' I heard him mutter.

'I hope he'll be all right,' I said to Julian when we were in the car.

'What on earth is a nice girl like you doing with a fellow like that?' asked Julian. By the tone of his voice I could tell that he wasn't entirely joking.

'Actually, he's quite nice when he's sober. He's extremely clever.'

'I wasn't exactly bowled over by his witty repartee this evening,' said Julian.

'He isn't really the witty repartee type,' I said.

'Then what sort of type is he, Julia?' Julian gave me a searching sidelong glance across the driving wheel.

'Oh, for Christ's sake, is this the Inquisition? Can't I even walk down the road with a friend without having to account for my movements?'

I answered sharply because the whole evening had put me on edge. The shrill ringing of the unanswered telephone was still fresh in my mind and I now felt stung with remorse.

We drove on in uneasy silence.

At last we pulled into my drive. Julian leaned over and kissed me on the cheek.

'Look, you don't have to go out with people like him just because you're lonely. I'll come over and take you out sometime.'

'Thanks, Julian, but you don't want to be landed looking after your brother's girl.'

'That's what you think,' he said with a broad wink.

By the next evening I was literally praying that Paul would ring. At last the phone shrilled out across the dark garden.

I hurried inside and lifted the receiver.

'Hallo.'

'Darling . . .' I loved the sound of Paul's voice.

'Hallo.'

'How are things?'

'Fine.'

'Still love me?'

'No, gone right off you as a matter of fact.'

'No, seriously.'

'Of course I do.'

'I rang you last night.'

'Oh . . . did you?'

'Where were you?' There was the tiniest hint of an edge in his voice.

'Out . . . I went to a party.'

'Have a good time?'

'Not very. It was a pretty awful party as a matter

of fact. I was rescued by Julian and he brought me home.'

'I know . . .'

'You've spoken to him.'

'He rang this morning.'

'Then you knew where I was last night.'

'He mentioned meeting you.'

'Why did you ask where I went if you knew . . .?'

'Julia, what's going on between you and that Polish chap?'

'Nothing. Absolutely nothing. He's just a friend.'

'Does he feel the same way?'

'Yes. No . . . I don't know . . . Yes, I think so.'

'Apparently he's a very subtle type with women . . .'

'Zig . . . subtle! What on earth is that meant to mean?'

'Well . . . girls kind of go for him.'

'I think you must have the wrong person.'

'Well, you don't, do you?'

'Go for Zig? Of course I don't.'

'So aren't you being a little unfair to him?'

'Unfair? How?'

'Leading him on.'

'Leading him on. I like that. All I've been trying to do is get rid of him. Hold on a moment.'

I could hear from the sounds in the kitchen, or rather the lack of sounds, that my mother must be listening in. I took the phone into the bedroom and closed the door.

It was then then we had our first full-blown row.

Dear Zig,

I tried ringing you but your phone seems to be still out of order. I'm sorry about rushing off on Saturday but you were in a bit of a state! And this letter has got nothing to do with that.

70

It's very hard to write this but I really don't think it's a good idea if we see each other any more. Everyone seems to think we've got a big thing going and you know and I know it's not true. Paul and I had a terrible row about it tonight.

I'm really sorry not to see you again but I think perhaps that's part of the trouble and it shows. This must sound terribly confused.

So please don't try and get in touch or come up here any more. I know my mother and father will be sorry not to see you and would send their love if they knew I was writing.

Please work hard and don't drink too much because I know one day you are going to do or write something really fantastic and I look forward to trying to read it.

With love, Julia.

I folded the letter carefully and found a handkerchief. I wasn't crying, I just had a terribly runny nose. I wrote Zig's address on the envelope and found a stamp and went out and posted the letter right there and then in the middle of the night. And so it was done.

It was oppressively hot that night. My room had a full-length door that opened on to the front of the house. At night I was instructed to keep this locked for the sake of security. But this night, finding I was still unable to sleep at two in the morning, I climbed out of bed and propped the door open so that a welcome draught of fresh air blew in through the inner mosquito wire door. I fell alseep to the restless sound of the plantains shifting in the rising wind.

The wall-eyed barman stood polishing the glasses, replacing each with a brittle clink on the mirrored shelves behind the bar. I shifted on the bar stool, crossing immaculate leg over immaculate leg. As I leaned forward to light the cigarette held delicately between my perfectly glossed lips, he took the lighter roughly from me. He lit the cigarette and watched as

71

I dragged on it and shook the gleaming swathe of blonde hair out of my eyes.

It was hot in the bar. The rotary fan hardly seemed to dredge its way through the torpid tropical air. Outside I could hear the palms moaning ominously.

I rose from the stool and, smoothing the tight skirt down over my hips, sauntered aimlessly over to the piano.

'There's a storm brewing up. Makes me kinda noivous,' droned the barman.

I opened the piano and played a single poignant note. The sound hung on the air like the last ring of a phone shrilling in the night.

At the back of my mind I could see Paul's car speeding along the Corniche. I prayed that he would reach the ferry before the storm broke. But a girl could rely on Paul. He would come into the bar and run a hand round my waist and murmur between his teeth.

'It's been too long not seeing you, doll.'

With a crash, the shutters flew open and the first breath of the storm came blasting through the room.

The wind tore at the palms and the surf broke high over the jetty. I was cold with foreboding, but I couldn't let the tension show. I just smoothed the folds of my taut crêpe de Chine blouse, and lit another Marlboro.

I could hear movements in the room above and I knew time was running out.

They rang for the barman and as he limped up the stairs I took my chance. My immaculately varnished nails slipped in the dial, as I fumbled with the coastguard's number. But it was no use. The phone was dead.

Now the rain was slashing across the windows, the wind howled and whipped at the thin weather-

72

boarding of the hotel. And as the full torrential force of the storm broke, I could hear the rain thundering on the roof.

A shot rang out. The door above flew open and the barman staggered out clutching his stomach. At the top of the stairs he paused, looking down at me, glassy-eyed, then he spun round sickeningly and falling, slid down the length of the stairs to a halt at my feet.

I screamed, a useless soundless scream, mouthed into the storm-filled air.

And then there was an urgent rattling at the door. I ran to it but I couldn't get it open. I knew Paul was the other side. Wildly I flung back bolt after bolt, the key turned in the lock but it wouldn't unlatch, I tore at the door, futilely turning the knob which swivelled loose in my head . . . And all the time the door rattled . . .

'Julia.'

I struggled to wake up. Paul's voice sounded strange, strangled, they had done something to him . . .

Then suddenly I was wide awake.

With an icy wave of realisation I found the rattling sound was real, it was my door being rattled.

'Julia,' the voice was more urgent.

I climbed out of bed and groped for my bathrobe in the dark.

His outline could just be made out dark against the mesh of the mosquito door.

'What on earth do you think you're doing here, in the middle of the night?'

'I'm wet,' said Zig in a muffled sort of way. 'Look, I'm drenched through.'

Peering through the netting I could see water actually running off him.

'What do you want?' I asked.

'I came to say I was sorry about being so absolutely vile the other night.' His voice was slurred and I could tell he'd been drinking again.

'Zig, for God's sake, it's the middle of the night.'

'You said that before. Look, aren't you going to let me in.'

'No, I most certainly am not.'

'Look, I'm drenched through. I'm shivering. I used to have a weak chest, you know. What if I died of pneumonia and it was all your fault?'

I could see he actually was shivering.

'Oh, all right, I suppose I'll have to let you in. But listen, my parents are asleep next door. You'd better go round to the front door and I'll come and open it. But don't make a sound.'

'OK.'

'And Zig . . .'

'Yes?'

'Nothing.' I had meant to say 'paws off', 'no messing around', but somehow I couldn't find the right words.

I let Zig in very quietly and I led him down to the kind of greenhouse affair that had been built on to the back of the house and was called the 'sleep-out'.

Zig was so wet he sort of squelched along behind me.

'You're going to have to get out of those wet clothes,' I observed.

'I know,' he said, smiling to himself in a self-satisfied sort of way.

'You've been drinking,' I accused him.

'That's right,' he said unrepentantly, and he started to fumble with the buttons of his shirt which was clinging to him.

'I'll make you some black coffee and find you something dry to put on.'

Why had I let him in? Why? I asked myself.

'No need,' said Zig, sitting down abruptly on the old sofa-bed, 'Never sleep in anything anyway.'

'Who said anything about sleeping here?'

'You can't send me out in weather like this!'

'You came in weather like this.'

By this time Zig was starting to take his trousers off.

'For goodness' sake, Zig, you can't just undress with me standing here. Stop it.'

I dropped my voice slightly, suddenly realising that at any moment my parents might wake up. It was rapidly becoming one of those situations that are terribly difficult to explain.

'You know something, you're a terrible prude,' said Zig.

'I'll get your coffee,' I snapped.

It took time to make the coffee quietly. I had to hover over the kettle in case it whistled.

It was very quiet when I got back to the sleep-out. Zig was lying stretched out on the sofa-bed breathing loudly, his trousers half-on and half-off, caught by his socks and sneakers which were still done up.

I crept over and shook him firmly. He just groaned and smiled.

'Lee-me-lone,' he mumbled.

Further shaking and complaining as loud as I dared equally failed to wake him.

I hesitated. It would serve him right if he slept in those wet things and caught a dreadful chill. Then I thought of what my mother would say if she found him like that in the morning.

So I took off Zig's filthy sneakers for him, and peeled off his wet socks, thinking at the time that he really did have the most disgustingly unattractive feet. And I even had to haul off his sodden trousers! Thank goodness he was wearing decent underpants.

75

Then I carefully tucked the blankets over him, trying to make him look as respectable as possible.

Gathering up his wet clothes, I crept quietly out of the room, turning off the light as I did so.

'Aren't you going to kiss me goodnight?' Zig's voice came from the make-shift bed.

I woke to find my mother standing over me.

'Julia, what's Zig doing asleep in the sleep-out?' she asked accusingly.

'He got caught in the storm. I had to let him in, he was soaked.'

'Well, I hope nothing went on,' said my mother, giving me a meaningful searching look.

'Went on? What, me and Zig? Don't be silly, Mummy. Honestly, your generation have only one idea!'

'I suppose I'd better give him breakfast then.'

I climbed out of bed, wondering whether Zig would be in a fit state to eat breakfast.

I had to wait for my shower as Zig took ages in the bathroom. He was singing! When he came out I could smell that he had helped himself liberally to my father's after-shave.

'Morning, gorgeous,' he said when he saw my blotchy un-made-up face. My mother gave us significant, suspicious looks from behind the teapot.

I just frowned at him and kept the breakfast conversation to the minimum.

The storm had blown itself out in the night, but it was still raining in a half-hearted way. It seemed Zig and I both had lectures so we had to catch the eight-thirty bus.

Zig dutifully helped my mother clear the table as I went to find my mac.

'Mummy, where's my mac?' I could have sworn I last saw it hanging in the corner of my cupboard.

'What mac?'

'My old Burberry.'

'It's hardly raining, Julia. You won't need a mac.'

My mother had never liked the Burberry, which was a man's I had bought second-hand. I was very fond of it.

'Yes, but where is it?' I asked, searching along the rail of clothes.

'Probably there somewhere,' she said with deliberate unconcern. 'You'll miss your bus if you don't hurry.'

'It's not, you know.'

Then I caught sight of my mother's face.

'You've given it away, haven't you?'

'I didn't think you'd need it, darling, not with the summer coming and then we could get you a nice new one back home. I'm trying to cut down on things to pack . . .' she ended lamely.

'Who did you give it to?'

'Ethel, actually.'

Ethel was our diminutive cleaning lady. I tried to imagine her in a man's Burberry.

'Then you'll have to get it back. Anyway Ethel couldn't possibly wear that mac, she'd be swamped.'

'It wasn't for her, it was for her daughter. She's in need of things at the moment.

'I'm in need of things too. My mac to be precise.'

'Yes, but she's in trouble,' she said significantly, then added when I still looked unimpressed, 'She's an "unmarried mother".'

My mother mouthed the last two words so that Zig shouldn't hear. It was a condition my mother still found rather shocking.

'I don't care if she's a pregnant nun. She's not having my Burberry, she should have been more bloody careful in the first place. There is such a thing

77

as contraception after all. For God's sake, isn't the world over-populated enough as it is? You'll just have to say it was a mistake and ask for it back.'

'Really, Julia, you'd think a girl of your age could have a bit more common humanity.'

'Well, I haven't, that's all. I'm sick of you giving my things away to every hanger-on.'

Zig was standing with his back to us looking out of the window during this conversation.

When I saw his expression I suddenly wondered if perhaps I had hurt his feelings talking about hangers-on.

We walked to the bus-stop in silence. He leaned against it moodily.

'Your mother's all right,' he said at last.

'I know,' I said. 'It's just that she's always giving all my things away. It gets on my nerves.'

'Possessions shouldn't matter,' he said. 'Things, they just weigh you down. Look at all these guys living round here, trapped in the treadmill of respectability. Four weeks grudging freedom per annum. That's what possessions do for you.'

I agreed with him in a way, but it wasn't the materialism of this little suburb that oppressed me, it was its uniformity. I watched one of our well-dressed young neighbours herding children into her car and driving off, as I had seen her every morning.

'It was only a second-hand Burberry,' I said apologetically.

The postman was working his way down the road on his bicycle slipping letters into those letter boxes that stand like miniature conning towers at the end of each Australian garden.

'I wrote to you last night,' I said.

'Rather a formal way to communicate, considering,' he said.

78

'Before you arrived, you idiot. I posted the letter, so I suppose you'll get it this morning.'

'It'll be a nice surprise then.'

'Don't you want to know what was in it?'

'Nope. That'll spoil the surprise. Love letter was it?'

'Zig for goodness' sake. Do try and be serious.'

'OK, I'm listening, but it still seems a pity to spoil all that effort you put into writing.'

At that moment the bus arrived.

We climbed inside with difficulty. The bus was packed. I was crushed against Zig. It was one of those silent, ruminative sort of morning crowds, people full of cornflakes and news bulletins, still rubbing the sleep out of their eyes.

'Gosh this is nice,' he said. 'By the way, you must have had difficulty getting my trousers off last night? I meant to thank you over breakfast.'

I flushed scarlet as several pairs of eyes turned on us.

'Zig, for goodness' sake,' I hissed.

'So what was in the letter?' he asked. 'I'm sure everyone would love to hear.'

'It doesn't matter. You'll find out soon enough when you get it,' I said wearily.

'You couldn't give me the tiniest clue?'

It was at about that time that we arrived at the Sinclair Street stop. Zig had to call in for some books, so he was getting out.

As he left I said: 'Zig, I'm tired of playing this game. I'm sorry. I'm really sorry.'

As I walked to lectures that day, a lot of figures in the distance had the irritating habit of looking like Zig. But when I got closer I was relieved to see they weren't.

The philosophy lecture hall was a temporary build-ing with an iron roof. By mid-afternoon the heat was building up inside. I tried to concentrate on what the lecturer was saying:

'Othello's judgement that Cassio loves Desdemona differs from his judgement that Desdemona loves Cassio, in spite of the fact that it consists of the same constituents, because the relation of judging places the constituents in a different order in the two cases . . .'

Why did everything have to come back to the same old subject? Love . . . love . . . love! Even Bertrand Russell seemed to have conspired against me to distract and send my thoughts wandering.

At last I judged by the depth of paper on the lectern that the lecture was drawing to a conclusion. I made a final futile effort to get down some meaningful notes.

There was the usual crush trying to get out of the hall. I didn't hurry; gathering my papers together slowly, I was content to leave with the stragglers.

Emerging into the dazzling afternoon light, I became aware of a tall loose-limbed figure, lounging cowboy-fashion, hands in pockets, against the lecture hall wall.

Zig slowly raised himself to an upright position and ambled up beside me.

'I thought for a moment you'd missed the lecture,' he said.

'Didn't you get my letter?' I asked.

'Letter? Yep . . . that's why I came.' He patted his pocket and smiled.

'But I specifically said I didn't want to see you again,' I hissed so that the 'first-years' ahead of me wouldn't hear.

'That's what you *said*,' he said. 'But it's not what you implied.'

'Oh, so what did I imply?'

Zig paused for a moment, he thrust his hands deep into his pockets and swung round to face me.

'Your letter *implied* that you really find I am disturbing your notions of what it should all be about with your stuck-up little luvvy-duvvy romance with your friend out East.'

'What do you know about it, anyway?' I replied hotly.

'All I know is that it's all very convenient having a whole bundle of emotions dumped on someone who is nicely out of the way so you don't have to commit yourself. So you can have a sweet romantic tight-arsed soft-lights-sweet-music affair that doesn't mean anything.'

I stared at him.

'Go away. Just go, I never want to see you again as long as I live,' I said. My voice was uncomfortably harsh with holding back an emotion I could not put a name to.

'I'm going,' he said. 'Perhaps one day if you ever come to live in the *real* world we might get to know each other.'

'What's up?' asked Glen, who found me patching up my face in the girls' room.

'I've just had the strangest kind of row with Zig.'

'I didn't know it was that kind of affair,' said Glen.

'But it's not, we're just friends.' I had to smile at the irony of the whole thing. 'At least we were.'

'Oh well, chin up, I told you he was a weirdo. Say, have you seen the new guy in the French group, the one who wears the black leather jacket?' And she was off again.

It was about then that things started to fall into that terrible accelerating downhill rush you can't avoid before any major journey. First we were going East,

81

where Paul would join us for a blissful week. And then we were taking the ship back to England. But before that, I had to take the end of year exams. I had left end of year revision far too late and was forced to spend hours working into the night.

Thanks to Zig's coaching, the Philosophy exam didn't seem to go too badly. And working on the principle that in French you only get marks off for your mistakes I kept my French essay in the present tense, for 'dramatic effect' of course.

The day before the English exam I went to a final lecture on Jane Austen's *Emma*. I arrived late and sat at the back of the lecture hall. From the steeply raked seats I could get a view of the main avenue that led down between the different faculties.

'We can, of course, compare the structure of the novel with that of classical drama.' The lecturer paused. I gazed absent-mindedly out of the window.

'Emma is blind to her own nature and cannot achieve enlightenment until she has . . .'

There he was, walking along slowly, with a girl! I craned over the heads of the row in front.

'Just as Oedipus cannot "see" the truth until his eyes are put out, so Emma . . .'

She was really quite a pretty girl. Slightly Asian, probably of mixed parentage. They seemed to be deep in some discussion. I felt a sharp pang of jealousy. Yes, real unadulterated jealousy, as they disappeared from sight.

'So it is with Emma. She is not enlightened and cannot "see" where her true affections lie until she comes to know herself.

'Thank you, that will be all for today. The next lecture will not take place until the new semester. So, until then, I wish you all success in your exams and a good and restful holiday after your exertions.'

I realised crossly how little of the lecture I had taken in. And it was all Zig's fault!

The morning of the English exam dawned with predictable perfection. My father drove me down to the University. I gazed blankly out of the window. I had never felt so uninspired in my life.

Poinsettia flamed callously against the clear blue sky. The road threw off mirages, little lilac pools that evaporated as we drew near. Emma, in her cool damp English drawing-room had never seemed further away.

'It's pointless,' I said to myself.

'What's that?'

'Nothing.'

There was a tense queue standing outside the Examination Room. I joined them, checked my watch and then stood there trying to disassociate myself from the whole thing.

We were ushered into the room. The windows were flung wide open for the sake of coolness, the air was bright with birdsong. No one should be expected to sit an exam on a day like this.

I selected a desk. Not too near to the front, or you feel you're being overlooked. Not too near the back or you see too many bent heads ahead of you.

The examination paper lay, smugly pink, face down on the desk. Before me stretched the long virgin foolscap sheets, clean, glossy and minutely flecked with tiny woody hairs that hint at the paper's origin so enticingly far away on some fir-clad mountain slope.

'You may turn over your paper now.'

The room was filled with the anxious susurration of papers turning in unison.

I dutifully read through the questions.

83

'Only connect. Give your views on the relevance of these words to any two of Forster's novels.'

Only connect . . . only connect. Nothing connected in my mind.

Further questions seemed equally meaningless. Everyone else in the room appeared to be writing feverishly.

'Just write a plan and you will be that much nearer to the afternoon on the beach with Glen.' I bribed myself.

The pen refused to write. I watched it with total detachment as it scrawled across the page. It wasn't my writing, it was a sequence of crabbed spidery marks that I didn't recognise.

In my mind's eye I could see the examiner trying to decipher it. I put down the pen and gazed out of the window. I only had to stand up and walk between those silent rows of tables and I would be out there standing warmed by the sunlight. I imagined the unturned faces watching me. I made as if to rise but I couldn't. I just couldn't force myself to stand.

So, if you're stuck here for three hours, you might as well write as not write, I told myself. At least it will help to pass the time.

'So how long did you sit there, you dope?' Glen rolled over on her back and massaged suntan lotion slowly across her stomach.

'Hard to tell. I didn't dare look at my watch.'

'Think you've got any chance of passing?'

'I might just have scraped through.' I pulled my sunhat over my eyes and breathed in the scent of warm straw now imbued with Ambre Solaire.

'Jeez,' she said. 'After all that work, too.'

'No need to rub it in.'

'Your folks going to be mad at you?'

'I doubt it. Look, do you mind if we talk about something else?'

There were a few moments' silence. Then Glen rolled over on her side nearer me.

'Listen,' she said. 'I gotta tell you something.'

I could hear from her voice that an intimate-confidence was on its way, so I pushed back my sun-hat and turned over.

'Promise you won't tell a soul?'

I promised.

'Absolutely swear it?'

I could see Glen was simply bursting to tell me, so I swore too.

'Well, Jack and I did it last night.'

'Where?' I said, rather irrelevantly. I knew just how strict Glen's parents were.

'On the back steps,' she whispered.

'On the back steps! What outside? All the way?' I said disbelievingly.

Glen nodded.

I tried for a moment to imagine Jack with his ginger hair and reddish skin and Glen doing it. On the back steps too.

'Did he have a you-know. I mean you're not going to be pregnant or anything . . .'

'No, but I've got the curse today.'

'That was a bit of a risk, wasn't it?'

'OK, so maybe it was.' Glen was obviously a bit put out by my reaction.

'So what was it like?' I asked, trying to sound impressed.

'It was all right,' she said. 'I'm going for a swim. Coming?'

I watched Glen's receding form as she made her way down the beach. She had that pinkish blotchy skin that was difficult to tan and she didn't have particularly good thighs. Once again I tried to imagine her and Jack making love on those rickety wooden steps behind the house. I didn't like the idea. I didn't like it at all. I suddenly felt very alone left there lying on the beach with all those bronzed bodies around me.

Chapter Eight

Zig: I was starting to formulate a theory. If you build up a great big bundle of emotions about someone and they kind of don't play along with it, they let you down, that bundle doesn't just go away. Oh no, that would be too easy. You're stuck with it right till you can just dump it down on someone else.

I was going through a pretty bad phase, drinking a lot and bumming the money for it off Leon and Bragge. Bragge had even resorted to coming out without any money because he knew if he had any, I'd just bum it off him. Sounds pretty mean, but I didn't blame him.

I got to thinking a lot about Julia. About her going away. About her going East and seeing that precious boyfriend of hers.

I was thinking about this one evening, sitting in a bar in town. It was a pretty disgusting bar. The kind of bar where they didn't swab the slops up much and when they did it was with a rat-grey grease cloth that kind of merged them all together. I liked the place. No one I knew was going to come through the door, and most of the other guys there looked as though they used the bar for the same reason. It was a loner's bar.

It was one of those nights when the heat kind of presses in on you. It was pressing really heavily, particularly inside in the bar. There was some kind of old-fashioned rotary fan but it hardly moved the air, it was that heavy.

It must have got to closing time because the guy who wielded the grease cloth came over, he shook me with his rat-grey hand and said:

'Come on, mate. Time to go home.'

I didn't like the feel of his grey greasy hand and I brushed it off kind of roughly.

'Take it easy, kid.'

He was a small guy and I could see he didn't want trouble.

'OK, mate,' I said. 'I'll go quietly.'

Outside in the street, I took a deep gulp of the thick hot air and set off for Sinclair Street. Then, all of a sudden, the rubbish that was strewn down the side of the pavement started to stir. Restless sheets of newspaper scuffled up to my feet and started kind of trying to wrap themselves round my legs. I turned and at that moment I caught the first blast of the storm full in the face. I stood still, resting against the hot breath of air that came forcing its way through the cloth of my shirt, cooling the damp bits of sweat on my body. Then I turned and ran with it like a kid.

I ran downhill with the wind, so that it felt like I was running so fast I wouldn't be able to stop, ever.

Then the rain came. At first, big hard individual lumps of it were flung out of the sky, hitting my back and running down against the hot skin inside my shirt. Then it came in great swathes. Sheets of it, drenching my body and running into my shoes. I stopped where the highway swept round out of the city and turned my face up to the sky and let it pelt down into my eyes and mouth. Water was skittering over the pavement, spitting up chutes of spray, spewing into the gutters, guzzling down into the drains. Then the first flash of lightning split the sky across and I waited for the thunder to roll.

One . . . two . . . three . . . four. Then a great vibrating rumble that seemed to rattle the buildings down to their foundations.

The rain had sobered me up. I could feel those old arteries pumping away, I wasn't going to sleep tonight. So I started walking. Walking in the rain. Walking until I had walked out all those grey areas that kept veiling their way across my precious thinking processes.

I didn't intentionally choose to walk up the Highway. Once I had passed Sinclair Street, I just kind of kept going. It must have been about 1.00 am when I hit Floreat Park and it had been raining hard all they way.

Once I was there I was kind of drawn to Julia's house. I started to think maybe the storm had woken her and I just wanted to check if there was a light on or anything.

Boronia Crescent looked pretty dead. The wind had dropped and the rain just kept on coming down, vertically drumming on the roofs. I started to shiver. It was bloody freezing standing there wet through; even my feet were wet.

I crept over their front lawn and I felt kind of funny about it in case someone took me for a burglar or something. Then I noticed that Julia's door was open. Her room had a door that actually opened on to the front lawn, not safe if you ask me. It had a secondary wire mesh door, which was closed, but it still didn't seem safe.

I was really shivering now. I rattled the door just quietly. Enough to wake her up, but not enough to wake her parents who slept in the next room. Why the hell didn't she wake?

Then there was a sudden movement in the room. Her face appeared at the door. She was wearing baby-doll pyjamas. That killed me, baby-doll pyjamas!

'What do you want?' she asked accusingly.

Now why do females always assume that if you catch them under-dressed you want to lay them? Nothing could have been further from my mind. I was too bloody freezing for a start.

I had to pile it on thick to get let in. All that jazz like apologising about being a bit over the top the night of the party etc. She wouldn't let me in through the bedroom door, though. I had to go padding round to the front. When she opened the front door, I was a bit disappointed to find she'd put on one of those towelling robes all done up tight round the neck.

She spotted the fact I'd been drinking. I guess my breath must have been pretty vile. We had to go pussy-footing round the house in case her parents woke up. Honestly, I don't know what the fuss was about. Henry was a real good guy. He wouldn't have minded me coming round, he probably would have given me a beer.

We got down into a kind of back-extension room they had which was built on to the house, and she was still giving me those sort of frightened-rabbit looks, as if I was going to leap on her or something.

I could see that if I made the tinsiest move I was likely to get thrown out into the night again. The callousness of the creature! So I decided to play along with the drunken bit. I mean I'm quite a big sort of fellow, a girl her size wouldn't have a hope in hell of throwing out a guy my size if he was nice and relaxed and unhelpful.

I started to strip off my clothes.

That did the trick, she disappeared in a flash and by the time she got back I had got myself bedded down in a kind of just-passed-out position on the couch.

She fell for it. She even finished taking my trousers off. That absolutely killed me. She tucked me up nice and tight and as she leaned over her hair just brushed very gently across my face. As she left, I couldn't resist saying:

'Aren't you going to kiss me goodnight?'

You never know your luck.

Daphne was very off in the morning, not herself at all, even though I'd showered and shaved and virtually drowned myself in after-shave. I'd really made an effort.

She and Julia had some sort of trivial argument about a mac and Julia said some pretty immature self-righteous things. She really could be pretty immature at times, especially when she was with her mother.

We walked up to the bus together and suddenly I got this vision of Julia fitting into the whole goddam system. She was only about five years off a Holden convertible with two kids and mangy dog in the back. She'd be married to some clean-cut guy who did something really creepy like dentistry and they'd make it in a sort of half-hearted clean-cut way once or twice a week. And I started to realise I didn't like the idea of any guy making it with Julia. Especially if he were some ego-tripping dentistry graduate.

Then in the bus she came out with all this stuff about having written me this letter. I tried to brush the whole thing off lightly because I could see by her tone what was in it. In the nicest way it would be telling me to get out of her creepy little clean-cut world because, 'Frankly, Zig, you don't fit in'.

So I kind of wasn't looking forward to going home. What made it worse was as soon as I got my nose through the front door my grandmother started bawling me out.

'Where have you been all night? I suppose you've been with that woman . . .'

I tore open the envelope.

'Don't you realise what night it was last night . . .'

Dear Zig,
     I tried ringing you last night but . . .

'It was a Thursday night. And what night is a Thursday night, my God . . .'

'. . . but I really don't think we ought to see each other any more . . .'

'Yes, Thursday night is Polish Union night. The only night I expect you to be in . . .'

Hell, it was too.

'. . . Paul and I had a terrible row . . .' Oh, it had to be Paul's fault, dear Paul.

'Don't you care? No, you don't care one little bit. The only night I like to be out to meet some people and where are you? Not in!'

I felt pretty bad about Grandma missing Polish Union night. All those old heads nodding over their lemon teas and poppy-seed cake and exchanging news from a place they still called 'home' . . . but I had to finish the letter.

''. . . to do or write something really fantastic and I look forward to trying to read it.'

And then at the bottom of the page there was this kind of inky splodge. I examined the splodge carefully and I read again the bit that went: '*sorry not to see you again and . . . I think it shows.*'

'And how do I know where you are? I sit here waiting in the night, and I started to think what will become of us . . .'

And I suddenly realised that I had made contact. Maybe she didn't know it yet. But somewhere deep down inside that little conventional soul of hers, Julia was capable of feeling . . .

I put my arm around Grandma.

'Babtia, Little Grandma . . . I'm going to make it up to you. I promise I will. One day we're going East and I'm going to find you a house with a real tiled roof and a washing machine and a garden with green grass and proper trees round. Big tall trees that drop their leaves every year . . .'

She knew the story, there was no need to go on. She sat down at the kitchen table with a sigh.

'Sometimes I wonder what will become of us . . .'

I put the kettle on and cut the lemon into fine slices and got out the sugar bowl filled with the fine white cubes of sugar and the silver spoons that Grandma always told me about: how she had kept them sewn inside her coat all the way down across goodness knows how many goddam hundreds of miles of Europe.

I put Julia's letter in my pocket and just for a moment with the sun streaming in through the open door and glinting on amber tea, I felt everything could be a lot worse.

Chapter Nine

Julia: 'Mummy, is it all right if I go to Ant's on Saturday?'

Anthony was on the phone. He'd invited some 'simply scrumptious' people round and he wanted me to help cook for them.

'You know we're going to the Sloanes'.'

We had started a dutiful round of farewell visits.

'But they won't want *me* there.'

'I accepted the invitation for all of us,' said my mother.

'Can't I be ill or something?'

'No, you most certainly cannot.' I could tell my mother was glad to have an excuse to stop me going to Ant's. She always imagined terrible orgies going on there. It couldn't be further from the truth.

Despite pleading, Saturday lunchtime found us on the way to the Sloanes'.

The Sloanes were my sister's in-laws. They had just moved to an architect-designed split-level house on the Boulevarde, one of the most fashionable up-and-coming streets in the suburbs.

My mother had had my white linen suit cleaned for the occasion and I had dabbed tennis white over the scuffed part of my white court shoes.

We admired the car-port and we discussed the number of miles per gallon Mr Sloane's new Ford could do. He gave us a demonstration of their underground piped lawn-sprinkler system, and he took us on a tour of the instant garden, which had come transported in plastic bags complete with its own topsoil.

I re-scuffed the shoes going up the mock Cotswold steps that led to the upper level of the house.

Sipping a glass of sweet sherry, I listened as my mother told Mrs Sloane how very hard I had worked for my exams and I told Mrs Sloane how I wasn't at all sure what I wanted to do when I left University and she said, reassuringly, that a girl like me would probably soon settle down.

I could see in her kind sort of way that she really wished me well and hoped that I, too, would one day have a car-port and a new Ford and a subterranean lawn-sprinkler system. And I gazed into my glass of sweet sherry and felt such a hypocrite coming out with all the right kind of platitudes.

At this point, my sister and her husband arrived with baby Katya and thankfully all the attention turned on the size and the shape of the baby and the noises she could make. So naturally, with all this attention focused on her, the baby started to cry and I offered to wheel her round and round the mock Cotswold path that led around that miracle garden, which had arrived in plastic bags complete with topsoil.

Then Mrs Sloane's younger daughter Janice came home. Janice made all her own clothes and she had done-terribly-well we were told in undertones while she washed her hands. She had a marvellous job in the big new hospital, which was a tremendous responsibility. Then we all agreed how terribly well young people did these days.

'Pineapple and pimento salad, dear?' Mrs Sloane's broad kind face inquired.

'Lovely, thank you.' I helped myself.

During the meal Mr Sloane told us about his job as a mining engineer.

'Yep, had the pipeline laid all the way to Kalgoolie and the night before they turned the water on they found him hanging in the bathroom.'

'More salad, dear?'

'Thank you. But why? Why should he do that just when everything he'd ever worked for was about to happen?'

'He just didn't have the faith that after ten years of work the water was actually going to get through,' replied Mr Sloane.

'Thousand Island or French dressing?'

'But that's terrible. It's so sad.'

I liked Mr Sloane and I didn't really take much notice of what Mrs Sloane and my mother were murmuring in undertones, until the passion fruit flan and lamingtons were served.

'What's all this I hear about a new young man,' said Mrs Sloane with a nod.

'What new young man?' I asked vaguely.

'Your mother says he's very clever. Studying Philosophy . . .' she said with another nod.

'Oh, Zig!' I said. 'What has she been saying? He's only a friend.'

'Not Zig Zuchelski?' said Janice.

'Yes, Zuchelski. If it's the same person.'

I couldn't imagine how Janice in her nice neat couturier-pattern clothes could possibly know Zig.

'Surely there can't be more than one?' said Janice.

'Hardly. What a character!' said my father.

'How do you know him?' I asked Janice.

'From the hospital,' said Janice.

'The hospital?'

'He brought his baby in when he was sick.'

'What do you mean, *his* baby?' I asked.

The room was very still. I watched the cake knife as Mrs Sloane eased it down between two slices of passion fruit flan.'

'Another helping, dear?'

'No, thank you.' Suddenly I wasn't hungry any more.

'Didn't you know about the baby?' asked Janice.

'What baby?'

'His baby. Didn't you know about it?'

'You must have the wrong person. Zig's only nineteen.'

'That's right,' said Janice.

'But Zig hasn't got a child. He would have told me.'

Or would he? I wondered. A lightning review of all I knew about Zig was running through my brian. Each glance, each nuance of speech, numerous unexplained details suddenly fell into place.

'What was wrong with the child?' asked my mother, making an obvious attempt to defuse the situation.

'Pneumonia. This was about three months ago. Zig just walked in with him wrapped in a blanket one Saturday night. The mother wasn't looking after the child properly. Or so he said.'

'Is the child all right?' my mother continued.

'Yes, but he was pretty bad for a time. There was a bit of a fuss because they hadn't got insurance or anything, so I got involved in all the admin. He should have told you . . .' she said.

'Why should he?' I asked.

'We got quite friendly,' Janice continued. 'I was on night duty and he used to come in every night and just sit with the child. I guess that's how in spite of his age he managed to get custody.'

There was silence for a moment. I watched a fugitive moth, caught between the net curtains and closed patio doors as it fluttered its wings against the barrier of glass.

'What a bombshell!' said my father and he laughed a sort of tight dry laugh.

'I said there was something odd about that boy,' my sister said meaningfully to my mother.

'Poor Zig,' was my mother's only response.

'Won't anyone have another slice of pie,' asked Mrs Sloane.

I think Katya, my sister's child, started crying about then and I offered to go and pick her up.

I stood in Janice's little white bedroom holding the baby and looking in the mirror. I stared at my reflection so nicely made up, so tastefully dressed in the white linen suit and I said to it: 'You bitch. You absolute bitch'.

I don't think I said much going back in the car. I don't think anyone did. I had this kind of yucky feeling in my throat that you get after drinking wine and eating sweet stuff at lunchtime.

So when we got home I said that if no one minded I was going for a walk. At the top of Boronia Crescent there was an untidy wooded bit. Not a proper wood like you'd get in England, but rough scrub that had just never been cleared because that's where the city ran out of houses.

They already had these posts staked out along the edge with numbers on them, so I suppose they were selling the area for building. I had to climb over some barbed wire to get to where the wooded bit was.

Inside, the trees grew tall and exposed with those kind of torn off unfinished bits you always get on Australian trees. There were black-boys dotted around here and there. Black-boys are stubby cactus-like tree things, they say they're hundreds or maybe it's thousands of years old, and they grow in kind of horizontal ridges. They're specially adapted to survive the constant drought-fire sort of existence a plant has to survive in Western Australia.

It was then, with a kind of jolt, I got this sensation

of time passing. Not time in the everyday sense, measured by calendars and watchfaces. But raw callous time, cold and mechanical, rolling smoothly from no beginning to no end. Time that stretched back without interruption in this dry cracked earth, where things had grown and died, evolving over millions and millions of years, long before there even was a human to tread there. And time stretching forward, approaching equally relentlessly with next year's bulldozers cutting into the red earth and uprooting the ragged trees and marking out the neat symmetrical lines of suburban streets. Lawn-sprinklers would soon be rotating over the elephant grass, and bronzed young housewives would be hanging out clothes on their rotary dryers. And their children would grow up and do the same, stretching the city out further and further. It would stretch on and on, endlessly repeating itself.

And here, right in between the two, was me, trapped in its total indifference.

I tried to think about Zig and I tried to work out what I felt about him and the child. I tried to remember all the stupid things I must have said, not knowing. And I told myself crossly that he should have been more bloody careful.

And then I thought of him walking into the hospital with the baby wrapped in a blanket and facing Janice, cool and well-dressed behind the desk. And I thought of all the damn foolish things Zig did the whole time. I knew I had to see him before I left.

So I walked back to Boronia Crescent and from the distance I saw my father fixing the latch on the garden gate so that he could lock up when we left. Bill Carr was leaning on his side of the fence talking to him. I could tell from the look they gave me that my father must have told Bill all about everything.

But Bill kind of just covered up as if he didn't know, the way he would.

'How you going?' said Bill. He always said that. He said that the very first day we arrived in the little white rented house.

He had leant over the fence and said:

'How you going? Come and have a beer.' And he'd been one of our best friends ever since.

'Look, me and your ma and pa are going to go up in the hills tomorrow to get a case or so of wine. You want come along?' said Bill.

I really wanted to see Zig but I knew tomorrow, Wednesday, he'd be working. His last exam, Metaphysics, was on Thursday, and he also had to talk to Selwyn about his dissertation.

'I'd like that, I really would,' I said.

I couldn't phone Zig, so I wrote him a note"

Dear Zig,
*   I'd love to see you before I leave. Can you make Thursday night? If so come up to my place 7-ish.*
*   Love Julia*

I tore it up. Knowing Zig, he might not even turn up.

Dear Zig,
*   I must see you before I leave. Could you ring me please urgently tonight. You know I'm going on Friday. Maybe we could do something on Thursday night?*
*   Love from Julia*

P.S. Best of luck with Selwyn.

Then I settled down to write a letter to Paul. I realised guiltily that I hadn't even thought of Paul for days. Still, in a couple of weeks we would be together. It didn't really give me the thrill it used to, thinking about it, but I guess that was because it was getting closer.

Next morning, on the way out of town, I asked Bill to stop at Sinclair Street and I dropped the letter in at Zig's place. It was pretty early, about 7.30 am and the house had a still, self-absorbed look about it. A window was open and a net curtain blew gently on the breeze.

I imagined Zig and the child sleeping somewhere inside and I suddenly felt that I had no place there. I made my way quietly up the cinder path and got back in the car.

There had been another freak storm during the night and as we sped out through the countryside the road was a bright terracotta colour, pockmarked with the force of the rain. A steady mist of condensation rose from it, evaporating in the sunlight. The dampness in the air smelt of fields and farms and I had never felt so aware of things growing.

It was a long way out to the hills and we soon left the farms and drove on through miles and miles of virgin bush. Bush with that particular stillness that is typical of Australia, a stillness only interrupted by the occasional flock of brightly-coloured cockatoos.

We reached the vineyards round about midday. There were mile upon mile of them, long parallel lines of vines describing the contours of the hills. Bill stopped the car and we all climbed out.

'Up there far as you can see,' he said, waving a wide red hand at the horizon. 'The land belongs to Mario and Marthe and the majority of it they cleared themselves, just the two of them, working side by side, adding a bit each year until they'd built up enough to hire themselves some labour. You won't taste a drop of wine like theirs in Europe. We keep the best for ourselves.'

'Come on, I'll introduce you.'

We drove up to a rambling homestead with a large handsome sign painted with the message:

'BLUE PEARL, pride of the West.'

'Marthe, I want you to meet some friends of mine. They're from England.' Bill leant over the counter casually as if he were in the habit of calling in every day.

'I looked at Marthe's small work-wasted body and wondered how she'd ever had the strength to work on the land. Her face was criss-crossed with lines, as if she were permanently looking into the sun.

'How's Mario?' asked Bill.

'Mario, he's in there,' Marthe jerked her head at the back room. The door was open and I could see a fridge and a kitchen table spread with an oilcloth in the gloom.

'He's crook,' said Marthe.

'Is he bad?' asked Bill.

'He's about as bad as he could be,' replied Marthe. Her mouth was firm and unemotional about it.

'What's wrong?'

'Nothing's wrong. He's just dropped his bundle, that's all.'

'I'll go in and see him,' said Bill.

And while Bill was gone, Marthe took us round to the wine store and she poured us each a glass of the fine cool white wine and Bill was right, you never got wine like that in Europe, not Australian wine.

When Bill joined us, he was very quiet.

As we left, he kissed Marthe and squeezed her arm. She shook hands with all of us. Her smooth hard hand felt as if it had been worn to a shine with work.

She said, 'See ya later,' to us. A phrase I never could get over, particularly since we were about to start on our trip back to England.

As we drove off, I looked back out of the rear window of the car and watched her as she stood at the gate, not waving or anything, just looking at the car, and then she turned and walked very slowly back to the house.

'What did she mean Bill . . . he's dropped his bundle?' I asked.

'It means, Julia, he's going to die.'

'But she said it with the door open and everything. Does he know he's dying?'

'Oh, he knows it all right. It's what he wants.'

'What's wrong with him?'

'There's nothing wrong with him. He's just had enough, that's all. Just like she said, he's dropped his bundle.'

I could see that I shouldn't ask any more. I gazed out of the window. It seemed totally inconceivable that on a day like this, with the sun virtually forcing life out of the earth, anyone could not want to hang to life for all they were worth until it was wrenched from them.

It was very late that evening when at last the phone rang.

'Julia.'

'Zig.'

'I got your note.'

'Good.'

'I can't make it tomorrow evening.'

'Oh.' I felt hurt, it was my last evening.

'How about tomorrow afternoon?'

'I was going to pack then but I suppose I could do it in the evening instead.'

'OK, fine. Where shall we meet?'

'I don't know. What can we do in the afternoon?'

'I'll think of something. I'll meet you in the Refectory about two-ish.'

'Zig?'
'Yes?'
'How did it go with Selwyn?'
'Not bad.'

Chapter Ten

Zig: You take it for granted, having a telephone. People just call you up and say, how's about doing this or that, and you just sort of make your mind up then and there, depending on how you feel. You never really think about it when it's there.

From where I was lying on the couch, I could see the place where the telephone used to be. My grandmother had put this vase of plastic flowers there so that the space didn't look so damn bare. You could tell from how much dust had collected on those flowers just how long it was since we didn't have a telephone. It was pretty thick.

Not having a telephone really destroys your privacy. I mean, people who would just call you up, turn up. Like Julia that time, just as I was in the middle of bathing Vlad. I had to leave him on the bed kind of half-wrapped up in a towel and all the time I was talking to her about beastly sweaters and things I could just about see him rolling off and half-killing himself and the Welfare people saying they'd been proved right.

Then Su turning up at the Metaphysics seminar that time she wanted money. If she'd rung, I could have just said straight out that frankly I didn't give a damn if she starved. Not any more. But as it was, I had to kind of humour her along till we got somewhere half-way private. I gave her some money anyway. She knew I would.

Then tonight, I got this letter from Julia. Could I ring her urgently because she wanted to see me tomorrow night. Tomorrow's Thursday. It's really ironic she should choose Thursday. Polish Union night. I mean we've had all this time to get it together and we get one last night before she kind of disappears into thin air and it has to be a Thursday. And it sounds like she's really keen to see me.

I wasn't going to ring from next door although it was an emergency, because I was pretty sick of Mrs-Next-Door listening in as if emergencies were kind of everyone's common property. I mean, the times I've had to give Bragge a list of whooping cough symptoms just to know if I could borrow a mangy fiver off him.

So I went down into town to call her up from the 'Prospectors', only to find that some joker had torn the phone right off the wall. That made me really mad so I had a couple of beers while I calmed down.

Down by the carpark there was this great queue of stragglers waiting for the call-booth. I was getting pretty desperate. By the time I got to a damn contraption that worked, it looked like she would be asleep or died of old age or something. It was a really slow queue. I kept giving the girl in the booth these really withering hurry-up looks and then the stupid cow thought I was giving her the come-on and started giggling and bawling down the phone to her friend about me.

I could have killed her.

Anyway, I just wasn't in a queuing up mood. So I gave her one last big really sexy wink just to make her evening, because she was a pretty ugly female and she probably hardly ever got as much as a glance from a guy half-way my standard. Then I walked all the way up and over to the campus to call her up on the pay-phone under the arches. It was pretty late by then. That's when I felt in my pockets and I realised that I had spent the goddamn change on the beer.

Of course there wasn't a soul around. No one hangs around the campus after about nine. Even the swots who use the library a lot, creep back under their stones at about nine-ish. And it was ten.

I considered making a collect call, but that was beneath

105

my dignity, especially after the way Daphne had behaved over breakfast the other morning.

Then suddenly I remembered the money in the cracked cup in the Common Room. We liked to have coffee in the Common Room and we kind of took it in turns to buy it. It was a nice relaxed kind of arrangement, only this real creep called Winterman kind of got the idea that it might be 'fairer' if we put in cash for the coffee. Kind of measured out the measly pence every time we had a miserly chipped cup full of the stuff.

God, some people are tight-fisted. Anyway, Winterman's hoard had come in handy before. The only question was how to get at it. The janitor would have locked up by now.

I made my way round to the back where the Common Room window was. There were these flower beds and some really dense shrubs, so I got pretty scratched. The windows were closed. I managed to force my penknife between two of them, but they were latched as well so there was no way I was going to get them to open. There was nothing else for it. I broke one of the window panes and then I climbed in.

The cracked cup was standing there, kind of wedged like a holy grail between the bottle of congealing milk and the sugar bowl full of hard coffee-soaked bits. I was in luck. It had some pence in it. It had two shillings as well. I left those. I'm no thief, not for two measly shillings, at any rate.

I was just about to get back out through the window when I heard this noise in the corridor and I kind of froze. I froze so hard that I knocked over the filthy milk bottle full of sour milk.

'Don't you move.' The janitor was shining his torch right in my eyes.

'Don't you try any funny business.'

'Hold on a bit, it's only me.'

'I can see who it is.' I'd come up against Kauffman before. He was one of those 'failed-the-the-SS-so-joined-security' type of janitors.

'You'd better come with me, mate,' he said, jerking his head towards the door.

I thought of trying to make a dash for it, but I kind of had the sense for once to see that that was only going to make things worse. Anyway, I was willing to pay up for the measly pane of glass.

He called Selwyn. *Selwyn*, over a mangy pane of glass!

It seemed like hours we had to wait for Selwyn. I had to sit in Kauffman's stinking office and look at his charts and calendars and things. Kauffman made himself a cup of tea but he didn't offer me one. All the time I was sitting there I kept looking at Kauffman's phone. In the end I decided I didn't mind if Kauffman listened into our blasted conversation, I was that desperate.

'Look, do you think I could use your phone, please?'

'No,' said Kauffman just like that.

'Look, it's only a goddam local call. I'll pay for it.'

'This is a college phone. It's strictly not for the use of the undergraduates,' said Kauffman. I could see he was getting a lot of satisfaction out of this.

It was just as well that Selwyn drove up at that moment. I could have just about killed Kauffman to get at that phone.

When Selwyn came in he looked all serious and un-Selwyn-like.

'Thank God you've come,' I said.

Selwyn didn't say much, he just kind of led the way to his study.

God the place was in a mess.

'Sit down, Zig,' said Selwyn, which was pretty unnecessary because I was already kind of spread across my favourite chair.

'Look, Selwyn, do you think I could possibly use your phone just for a minute. I've got this really urgent call to make, then I can explain everything.'

'I think perhaps we ought to talk first,' said Selwyn.

God he was making a big deal over a measly little incy-tincy pane of glass.

'You didn't need to do this, Zig. You of all people. I mean I really had hopes for you. I mean that dissertation was good. Bloody good. You could take tomorrow's paper in your stride with no problem.'

What was he talking about? What the hell was he going on about? Then suddenly it all dawned on me. Selwyn thought I had broken in to take a little private view of tomorrow's Metaphysics paper.

'Selwyn,' I said dead straight. As dead straight as I've ever said anything to anyone and I looked him right in the eyes. 'If you think that I would jeopardise all I've worked for just to have one miserly glimpse at a load of sodding questions you are wrong.'

Selwyn looked straight back. I could see he believed me.

'But, Zig,' he said slowly. 'Someone has. I mean someone's tried. They didn't succeed of course. We keep the papers locked away in Denise's safe. But someone's tried. Do you want to tell me what you were doing in here.'

'I needed some money.'

'You'll have to try harder than that, Zig. If you needed money you might well find robbing a financial institution, like a bank or something, rather more fruitful than a Philosophy Department.'

'No, you see I didn't need much money. I just wanted some of the change out of the cracked cup in the Common Room.'

'So how much did you take?' Selwyn frowned.

I took the money out of my pocket. 'Only three pence. The pound's mine.'

'You mean to say you broke into the building for three pence . . .'

'It was for the phone. The pay-phone under the arches. Look, please, Selwyn, let me make that call. It's only a lousy local call. I'll pay for it.'

Honest to God, I was so frustrated I was virtually crying.

'Help yourself,' Selwyn got up and he left me to make it alone, which was pretty decent of him.

Julia answered really quickly, I think she must have been waiting by the phone.

We didn't say much. I was kind of too shaken up to say much. Then right at the end of the call she said:

'How did it go with Selwyn?'

For a moment I thought she had second sight or something.

We went to the Zoo. I was in a really buoyant mood because that Metaphysics Paper in the morning was my last exam and I didn't think it had gone too badly. I hadn't even started worrying about whether I thought it had gone too well. I had also managed to extricate some money from Winterman. Winterman of all people! Winterman was just sitting in the Common Room looking kind of green and when I asked him for a loan, I kind of implied it was to pay Selwyn for the broken window. I vaguely suggested I was going to get sent down if I didn't have it. And he gave me this funny sort of look and said: 'That'll make two of us.' Then Selwyn called him in to see him about something.

She arrived right on time. That was one of the things I liked about Julia. If you planned to meet somewhere at a certain time, she'd be there. She didn't keep you hanging around just to prove how goddam special she was. She was wearing this blue and white striped dress thing. It looked really good on her. She generally wore jeans which looked pretty good on her too, but this blue and white striped dress thing had one of those wide necks. It was so wide you coud see just a bit of her shoulders so you could tell she wasn't wearing a bra or anything because it'd show. It was a really cool dress.

'That's a really cool dress. Is it new?'

'Yes, thanks. I got it to go East . . .' she paused and just a shadow of a frown seemed to cross her face.

'Where are we going?' she asked.

'To the Zoo,' I said it in a muffled sort of way. The Zoo

109

isn't kind of the most romantic place to take someone. It
smells a bit.

'Great!' she said. She was really pleased, she wasn't
putting it on at all, I could tell.

In order to get to the Zoo, if you didn't have a car, that is,
you have to cross the Swan River by ferry.

When we were on the ferry, she didn't want to go up on
deck where those slatted seats are all set out in respectable
rows for people to sit on. She said she'd rather go down on
the bit where the cars were, so that she could be really
close to the water.

So we stood right in the stern and once the ferry got
going, it thrust out this great boiling wake of foam. She leant
against the side staring down into it and I kind of casually
put one arm on either side of her and leaned over her
shoulder and stared into that boiling hypnotic water. She
smelt good. All freshly showered, not perfumy or anything.
I was just leaning down to kiss that really cool bit girls have
where their neck kind of joins on to their body, when she
said.

'I wish you'd told me.'

And then I realised she knew about Vlad.

I swung round and leant with my back to the wake so that
I could take a look at her face and know how she felt about
it.

'Who told you?'

'Janice. You know, my brother-in-law's sister. She works
at the hospital.'

Of course, dear cool efficient helpful Janice. Perth is
such a small town.

'Why didn't you tell me?'

'You never asked.'

'Seriously, Zig.'

'To start with there was no point. Then I nearly did, once.
But then it was too late because I'd kind of started covering
up. It doesn't do a lot for a guy's image, you know, having

a kid in tow.' It was surprisingly difficult to talk to Julia about it.

'Actually, I think it makes you seem kind of "strong-and-silent",' she teased.

'You don't feel too "strong-and-silent" when you're going to be a dad at seventeen.'

'Is that all you were?'

'Yep.'

'How old was she?'

'Twenty-six. Twenty-seven maybe.'

We had arrived at the other side of the river and I helped her climb over the piles of greasy ropes that were lying about the deck.

I think she could tell I didn't want to talk about it any more, so she just changed the subject. She started rabbiting on about the zoo and which animals she wanted to see.

I paid for the tickets and nuts for the animals. I wasn't going to let her pay for anything. Today was my treat. When we walked down the avenue that led to the cages, she slipped her arm through mine and she kind of squeezed my arm in a friendly sort of way and I could tell she was trying to make me feel less up-tight.

So I just relaxed and we did really childish things, like making seal noises at the seals till they all started barking like mad, and throwing peanuts so the monkeys could catch them.

She wanted to see everything. There wasn't a single animal that didn't get looked at and given a point-score for its sex-appeal. Wart-hogs are my favourite and we had an argument about that, because according to Julia they score pretty low, I mean, I pointed out a really cool stud of a wart-hog. He was really bristly. I bet he'd have to shave about three times a day and if I'd been a female wart-hog I really would have gone for him.

By about four, we decided we'd better get back. We just had about two peanuts left and Julia insisted on feeding them to one solitary black chimpanzee who was all alone in

111

a cage for some reason. He was looking pretty depressed about it, whatever it was.

She held the peanut and poked it through the mesh for him to take. I suppose it was rather a dumb thing to do, because instead of taking the nut, he just grabbed hold of her fingers.

It was only for a few seconds because I pulled her arm away, but it really shook her.

'His hand, his nails, they were just like human fingers . . .' she said.

So I took her hand in mine and put it in my jacket pocket and held it there.

We didn't say much on the return journey. We sat up on deck this time because there were more cars on the way back and they wouldn't let us down on the car deck. I would have liked to get up close to her and maybe to have started something, but there were quite a few other people there.

The sun was still shining, but low down, and it was getting misty. Everything was kind of muffled and grey. The nearer we got to the other side, this kind of dark greyness seemed to be closing in on me.

'I wish I didn't have to go tomorrow,' she said.

'For Crissake. It's a bit late to say that, isn't it?'

'Yes. But I wish I didn't,' she said.

I looked at her and her eyes had that kind of brimming look. I felt absolutely terrible too.

'You don't *have* to,' I said.

'Yes I do.'

'You'll be all right,' I said. I don't know why. It was a pretty daft thing to say.

'I know,' she said.

'And I'll be all right.'

'Yes, I know,' she said.

And I could hear that if she said anything else she'd start crying so I just shut up.

112

We didn't say anything all through town and in the bus we had to stand because it was the rush hour, of course.

It was getting pretty late.

'I'd like to see you home and say goodbye to Henry and Daphne, but I can't. You'll have to say goodbye for me. And thanks and all that.'

And she nodded and bit her lower lip.

When we got to Sinclair Street, we exchanged a really chaste little kiss on the cheek and I got off.

As the bus left I realised I'd never even once kissed Julia properly, not once. It was ironic really.

Chapter Eleven

Julia: It was a small black hand. Each finger finished with a perfect gleaming fingernail. A black fingernail, not pink underneath like people's are. The fingers gripped mine and for a moment I could feel myself . . . this sound crazy but it's the only way I can describe it. I could feel myself being pulled down into the past. A primitive past that was still there, waiting, just below the surface. I had a glimpse of it and than Zig pulled my hand away.

He just took my hand in his big warm one and held it inside his pocket.

'That better?' he asked.

Most guys would have just made you feel stupid for doing a dumb thing. But Zig didn't.

It was a good feeling. His hand was warm and dry. I liked Zig's hands.

On the way back in the ferry I was feeling really terrible. I had this massive lump in my throat that just wouldn't go down. I wanted to say something to Zig. While there was still time.

'I wish I didn't have to go away.' I had no right to say that, but it kind of slipped out.

'You don't have to,' he said.

It was getting cooler. A low mist seemed to be settling over the river, blurring the outlines of things.

No, he was right. I didn't have to go. I wished I could get everything clear in my brain. I couldn't see any future in staying. It was impossible. He was impossible.

114

So we said goodbye, crammed in a bus aisle with a jostling crowd of commuters. I kissed him on the cheek like a brother or something. And I realised we'd never even kissed each other. Not properly.

I had to stand all the way to Floreat Park. When I got out of the bus I felt pretty weak at the knees. I suppose it was the standing. I didn't feel wild about spending an evening packing, but it had to be done.

As I rounded the bend to our house I saw there was a car outside. Paul's car stood accusingly outside the house.

For a moment I hesitated, then realised that, of course, it was his mother visiting. Paul had always borrowed his mother's car, so much so that even she had started to refer to it as his.

I made my way slowly down to the front door.

'Julia, at last. Look who's here to see you,' my mother came to the door.

'Hello, Kathy,' I leaned down and kissed her on the cheek. I had forgotten how blue Paul's eyes were. Blue like Kathy's. 'It's so late and you've still got all your packing to do. Where have you been?' asked my mother.

'To the Zoo,' I said.

'The Zoo?' said Kathy. Nobody went to Perth Zoo. 'All on you own?'

'No, I was with a friend,' I said casually. 'Mummy, is there any tea in the pot?'

'Well, I don't know why you want to go rushing off to the Zoo on your last day of all days,' said my mother.

'Do you know I've lived here all these years. I've never once been to that zoo,' said Kathy.

'Would you like some fresh tea, Kathy? I'll make some more?'

From the kitchenette I could hear Kathy going on

about the Zoo. She was talking about the Zoo but she was wondering about the friend.

'So are you all set for your trip East?' said Kathy when I came back. 'I've brought some things for Paul and I've brought a little something for you.'

Kathy was holding out a black leather case. The kind jewellers give with a necklace or something.

I opened it. Inside was a little Edwardian pendant, set with blue gems, blue like their eyes, not my colour at all, really.

'It's only paste,' said Kathy, 'but I used to wear it when I was your age. I'd like you to have it.'

'Oh but, Kathy, you shouldn't. Really you shouldn't,' I said.

'I want you to have it. I know Paul would want you to have it.'

I thanked her and we talked about the trip and I could feel myself slowly and inexorably becoming enmeshed in the preparations.

'You don't *have* to go,' Zig had said.

But I did. It was too late to turn back now.

When Kathy left, I went to the door with her and she turned as she went out.

'There's always the beach house,' she said.

'The beach house?' I repeated stupidly.

'The beach house. If you and Paul . . . Well, it's always there and you're welcome to it. If, you know . . .' she squeezed my hand.

I spent the evening packing. I laid each garment flat, smoothing it out as I did so.

The dress I had worn the night I met Paul. My hair was coming down and he took out all the pins and it shook out over my shoulders. The loose cotton shift I used to work in. For a moment the wind shifted through the willows, and I was in the garden. I could hear the creak of the old wicker rocking chair. The crisp white linen suit: as I folded it I was again standing in Janice's bedroom gazing in the mirror and holding my sister's baby.

It was almost midnight when I finished. I lay in bed gazing into the darkness, chasing those little squiggly coloured bits you almost see in the dark but disappear when you look at them. I hadn't even bothered to undress, I knew I wouldn't sleep.

My door was being rattled.

'Julia.'

'Zig?'

'I couldn't sleep.'

'Nor can I . . .'

I undid the mosquito wire door and slipped out.

Zig just put his arms around me and kissed me properly, very gently.

'Don't,' I said, because I enjoyed it.

'What shall we do then?' asked Zig.

'Let's walk. I feel like walking. Let's walk down to the sea.'

'The ocean you mean.'

'Yes, the ocean.'

'What time are you leaving?'

'About seven o'clock I think.'

So we walked through the silent streets where the cars slumbered in their driveways and the houses lay, great dark somnolent shapes in their gardens, each with its little sentinel letter-box keeping watch.

We walked down the Boulevarde and I pointed out Janice's house, clean and white and architect-designed in the moonlight.

At the end of the Boulevarde we met the ocean. It always came as a shock, the power of those great rollers crashing in relentlessly, one following the other with hardly time for the water to heave itself back off the shore.

On the beach we took our shoes off and left them

under the beach sign and turned and walked off up the shore, the fine sand squeaking like snow under our feet.

'Europe's somewhere over there,' said Zig, pointing out over the ocean. 'I'll be able to look out there and know that's where you'll be. There's Julia, under the same sky, under the same old sun and the same old moon.'

'But under different stars,' I said.

And he reached out and grasped my hand in his big warm one.

'Know how far we could walk up this beach?' asked Zig.

'No.'

'About three hundred miles.'

'I feel as if we could just keep on walking like this for ever.'

'I couldn't,' said Zig. 'I'd have to get back to Vlad.'

'Doesn't his mother want him back?' I asked.

'No, she doesn't want anything to do with him. She's no good, you see. No good at all.'

'Is that why you didn't want to marry her?'

'Oh, I would have married her all right. She was the one who wouldn't get married. All she wanted was an abortion.'

'Then why didn't she have one?'

Zig looked at me:

'Don't you know anything? First of all it's illegal. And secondly, just supposing you can find someone bent enough to do it, think what it costs? I worked my arse off trying to earn enough to kill my own goddam child.'

'So why didn't she have one?'

'It kind of got too late. I would never have got enough together anyway and it got later and later. It just got too late. It's the story of my life really. I kind of leave everything too late.'

He had been walking more and more slowly while we were talking. And at that moment he stopped and said:

'Wait a minute.'

Then he kissed me again but not gently this time. And for a moment I forgot that this was only Zig and we were just friends and that I was going away, as the surf boomed on the beach and I could feel the soft cool texture of the sand beneath my feet.

'You're right. It is too late, Zig,' I said, gently pushing him away. But he didn't seem to mind.

That was the nice thing about Zig, he didn't go on like some guys would have, just to protect his male pride.

He just looked at me in that half-joking Zig-ish sort of way and said:

'Yes, I know. But it was worth a try, wasn't it? Come on I'll take you home.'

We got back about half-past six in the morning and my mother was going berserk. She was really livid and Zig had to calm her down in the kitchen. I don't know what he said but it seemed to do the trick.

We all had breakfast together. It was a pretty miserable meal, finishing things up, with the suitcases kind of piled in the hall.

Zig helped us load the car. My parents fussed over everything, but we did it in silence mostly, we were pretty tired by then. On a last look round the house my father found a bottle of whisky he had forgotten to pack.

That was the last thing I remember about Zig, the whisky I mean. We gave him a lift down to Sinclair Street. When we got to his house he said:

'Can you wait a minute? I won't be long.'

When he came out he was carrying Vlad. Vlad was

119

all wrapped up in a pink knitted blanket thing and he looked out in a sleepy sort of way. He looked very small in Zig's arms.

'He's beautiful,' said my mother.

'No, he's not, he's just like me,' said Zig. 'Rugged.'

But I didn't trust myself to say anything.

Then Zig handed me a parcel.

'Goodbye present,' he said.

'I haven't got anything for you.'

But my father reached under his seat and pulled out the bottle of whisky and said:

'How about this. Will this do?'

Zig looked at the bottle and said:

'This'll help.'

Zig: Vlad played up that Thursday night. I mean usually he's a pretty cool sort of guy. Great sense of humour and everything. He's got this vile neon pink sort of squeaking duck thing and generally you've only got to think of a really kind of unexpected time to squeak it and he just sort of creases up. He doesn't laugh much if you squeak it while he's watching. That's what I mean about his sense of humour. He's discriminating.

Anyway, that Thursday night, even the subtlest sort of neon duck work didn't raise a smile. Maybe I was a bit uptight when I got in. I was nearly late for Grandma leaving. She already had her coat and hat on and everything. She let rip a bit.

Maybe Vlad could tell that he wasn't really getting my full attention. He can kind of sense when you're not concentrating, if he's trying to communicate something. Anyway he just bawled and messed around with his food, so I put him to bed. And then he bawled a lot more.

It's pretty depressing being stuck in a house with a kid that bawls and no telephone.

The thing was, I wanted peace to think about this Julia situation.

'I wish I didn't have to go away,' she said. It was turning cool and her shoulders were going all sort of goosey in that cool wide-necked dress of hers.

'You don't have to,' I had said. I'd said it without thinking, but now I tried to think through what would happen it she stayed. I tried to think it through, Vlad crying like a maniac. I tried to picture Julia in that cool wide-necked dress of hers in the house. I couldn't find anywhere to put her. I couldn't see Julia washing up in the big white sink. I couldn't see her in Vlad's room, picking him up or anything. I couldn't even picture her sitting in an armchair, for Crissake.

I could only see Julia driving a big estate car with Vlad kind of sitting in the back strapped into one of those neat kid's seats, all dressed up and everything. Then I tried to think of ways this could come about. I kind of had some pretty ignominious thoughts about whether Henry might cough up for us. I mean, Henry kind of liked me, I knew.

Then I thought of Sundays. Henry and Daphne and Julia and Vlad and Grandma were all kind of cramped round a table in a house like Julia's house. I'd have some sort of job in some sort of dumb bank or something and have some sort of crappy Terylene light-weight to wear during the week. Then I thought of Vlad just killing himself over seeing me in a suit.

So I went and picked Vlad up and I realised I'd left him crying so long he was making those kind of hiccuppy shuddery noises trying to stop crying. I'd never left him that long before.

'We're not going to let them get us,' I said to Vlad. 'Oh no, we're not.'

Then Vlad tried to kind of force a smile right through all the tears and everything. He was such a cute guy.

He kind of calmed down after that. I propped him up on the sofa and read him bits of Grandma's Polish newsletter. It kills him if you talk to him in Polish. But he kind of dozed off after a while and I picked him up, very gently so as not to wake him, and put him back to bed.

But I couldn't sleep, long after Grandma got back and was tucked up in her little narrow bed in Vlad's room. She wouldn't sleep anywhere else, not since the day I brought him back from the hospital.

I kept thinking back. I thought back to the day that Grandma found out about Vlad. God, she'd hit the roof. It wasn't about the baby, it was about the abortion. She's a Catholic, a really religious Catholic. She'd made me get confirmed and everything. I'd been working myself sick and she faced me up with it one night. She knew why I had to get all that money. She just kind of guessed. I mean, Grandma's no fool, she must even have had a sex-life once. Well, she must have.

Then I thought about the way Grandma came round when the Welfare people wanted to take Vlad. She was fantastic. She just barged into that office, barged past the secretary and everything and just walked in, kind of dragging me along with her.

'He is *our* child. He stay our child,' she said.

She still doesn't speak English too well. They looked pretty surprised. I mean, I had to sort them out a bit about our relationship, Grandma and me. But she wouldn't back down. That's how we got Vlad.

Then my brain kind of frog-hopped from memory to memory, you know how it does, and I got to thinking about Julia again. I realised I hadn't said goodbye to her properly. She was going away in the morning and it was pretty damn certain I was never going to see her again. I mean after the Eastern States, they were going back to England. Unless she decided to stay on for that other guy. Either way, I wasn't going to see her again. Not ever.

I walked all the way up to Floreat Park, just to say goodbye properly.

I mean, I know I wasn't in love with the girl or anything, whatever that's meant to mean. I just had to say goodbye to her properly, that's all.

When she came out I thought I ought to kiss her. Well, I never had and I didn't want to give the poor girl a complex or anything.

I was careful to keep it one of those sort of non-passionate type of exploratory kisses. Girls like those. I don't kind of mind them either. I mean, kissing can be kind of disgusting at times.

Then we went for this massive great walk down to the ocean. I kind of like talking when you're walking. You don't have to look at people when you're walking along. We talked a lot. Perhaps during that walk I got to know Julia better than I had before. I was starting to see that there was a lot of Daphne and Henry in Julia, the good bits. It sounds crazy liking someone because of their damn parents and everything, but it's true.

We walked up the shore with our shoes off and the sand was cold and squeaked the way it does when you walk on it. She said it squeaked like snow. I've never seen snow, not to remember. Pretty ironic really, when you consider where I come from.

The ocean was really doing its bit. Crashing in on the shore like crazy as if it was trying to get back at the land just for being there. It was kind of sucking up great hunks of it and spewing it back. It reminded me of the times I used to sit and watch it as a kid and wonder how long it would take till it had kind of chewed up all the land and made everything sand. I used to think I'd be pretty old by the time it had. I guess Vlad will think of that sort of thing pretty soon.

'I feel as if we could just keep on walking like this for ever,' said Julia.

But I was thinking about Vlad and I said a pretty put-down-ish sort of thing – that I couldn't because I'd have to get back to Vlad.

But that's the nice thing about Julia, she never seems to feel put down by things like that.

We were talking about Su, but I was thinking about Julia. She was walking just this little bit ahead of me, so I was watching this really cool bit of neck girls have that really turns me on. I was saying something about always leaving things too late. I meant us, but I think she still thought I was just going on about Su and all that.

Then I meant to just kiss her gently but I was knocked out by the way she kissed back. I mean, really passionately. And with all that surf booming like crazy I really wanted to make love to her right there on the beach.

I even got as far as feeling in my pocket to see if I'd got something with me. I usually stock up from Bragge's drawer. He doesn't mind, I think he just gets a kick out of going out and buying them, poor sod.

But I hadn't. It was just my luck. But I wasn't going to take any chances, I mean, there are some mistakes you just don't make twice.

When we got back to Julia's place, Daphne was really mad. I think she thought we'd been making it all night or something.

So I just said to her in the kitchen,

'You think I've been making love to your daughter, don't you?'

This embarrassed the hell out of her.

'Well, haven't you?'

'No,' I said, 'But I wish I had.'

'Zig, you're impossible. You really are impossible.' That was all she said.

I think they were pretty glad they were getting Julia away from me in the end. Well, I don't blame them.

Julia: After we left Zig we drove for a long way in silence. I think I must have fallen asleep. When I woke up we were miles out of town, way out in the bush. Flocks of green gullahs kept on swooping down across the road and back into the bush. As I watched them I kept on telling myself:

'I don't love Zig. I really don't love Zig.'

Zig: After they drove off, I walked back into the house with Vlad and I sat him propped up by a cushion on the sofa. Then I went and got a glass and opened the bottle of whisky and poured half a tumbler and sat with Vlad and drank it. Then I poured another half tumblerful.

I didn't love Julia. I knew I didn't.

* * *

Julia: 'Aren't you going to open Zig's present darling?' My mother interrupted my train of thought. I had quite forgotten about it.

I slit open the brown manila envelope and pulled out a carbon copy of Zig's dissertation. Attached to it with a paper clip was a black and white photograph. I didn't recognise him for a second. It was a picture of Zig, dressed in a dark suit, holding a big bunch of white roses.

On the back was written: 'Sorry about the photo, it's the only one I've got. It was taken on my first communion.'

We wrote, of course, for a time. Zig's letters were full of news of other people, other girls. His letters were pretty non-committal really. Apart from, perhaps, the last one he sent. It ended:

'I still (though more rarely) wander in the early morning and feel extremely happy when I "hear" your footsteps beside me, but now I no longer hear the laughter in your voice.'